GW00361250

A SECOND CHANCE

— A MURDER MYSTERY —

JEROME RABOW, Ph.D.

ISBN 978-1-953223-37-1 (paperback)

Copyright © 2020 by Jerome Rabow, Ph.D.

All rights reserved. No part of this publication may be reproduced, distributed, or transmitted in any form or by any means, including photocopying, recording, or other electronic or mechanical methods without the prior written permission of the publisher. For permission requests, solicit the publisher via the address below.

Rushmore Press LLC
1 800 460 9188
www.rushmorepress.com

Printed in the United States of America

CHAPTER 1

Lost Love, New Love

Detective Joseph Zuma was in love. It was the second time. A hit-and-run driver had killed his first wife, Carol. Zuma was unable to accept that the police were never able to find the driver. Paralyzed by this state of affairs, he started to track down all drivers in Los Angeles who had received a DUI over the past three years and made them account for their whereabouts on the night she was killed. It was also during this time that his heavy drinking began. After a number of drivers complained to the precinct that Zuma had harassed them about their driving record, he was asked to take a leave of absence or go on sick leave for three months. He realized that his career was in jeopardy and decided to begin going to AA meetings. The meetings helped him be aware that a lot of hit-and-run drivers would not have a record. He was shocked to realize how naive he had been. He had gone to meetings for ten years and now he no longer attended. He felt in control of his drinking.

His father had told him that every man is entitled to at least one great love and that "Some of us who are lucky get a second chance."

He had seen Claudia a year ago when he was vacationing in Truro, Massachusetts. Now, one year later, as he was shopping in Truro, he remembered her and introduced himself. It was an instantaneous smoldering connection. It was not so much one of passion as it was the amalgamating of two metals to make something more brilliant. She was a landscape painter and her Vistas of Cape

Cod were many of the same ones he had loved to visit on bike or car before he met her. He loved space and he loved quiet. Her paintings of the landscapes at the Cape readily spoke to those exact preferences of his.

CHAPTER 2

A Proposal and a Safety Net

It was now nearing the end of his monthly vacation and his colleagues were expecting him back at work in the 25th Precinct in Santa Monica. He and Claudia had spent every night and day together. Some days she would paint, and he would just take a beach chair to be next to her and read. He would cook most evenings, taking advantage of the fresh catch of the day. Other times they took hour-long walks on the beach. One day, they had walked the six-mile, three-hour walk on the beach into Provincetown. Exhausted, they sat with sandy feet, drank white wine, ate mussels, and acted like all the other tourists who wandered the streets of what the natives called, "P Town." They went to the theater two different evenings in Wellfleet and Truro, and on one afternoon after much coaxing, Carol took him to the gallery where most of her art was in full display.

The gallery owner was quite proud of her.

"She's practically a native, you know. Many in town would disagree because they like to claim their families came here on the Mayflower. I don't know what they're so proud of. They turned on the Indians and didn't share their corn. They starved them or shot them after the Indians had taught them how to grow it. I consider her a native. I'm proud of her. She's lived here for twenty years and she shows our natural beauty to the world."

That's how Zuma thought of her—a natural beauty. They hadn't talked much about what was going to happen at the end of his holiday, but he decided to broach the topic

"I want you to come back with me to Santa Monica. I promise you that you will have lots of new and great vistas, and the colors in Los Angeles are different. We have great museums, a wide variety of eating-places and other places for us to hike in or just walk to. I have a big house. You can have your own studio. You don't have to give up your place here. You can hold on to it. I don't really think you will need it, but I understand safety nets. In my business, we have to have safety nets."

"What is that for?"

"Colleagues who we can count on when there is real danger."

"Oh, do you think I'm in real danger?"

Zuma laughed, "No, darling, I'm the one in real danger. I am hopelessly in love with you."

CHAPTER 3

The Native Leaves

Claudia had been scarred by betrayal early in her marriage. She had been an art student in New York, and her husband's affair with her close friend crushed her. She left the city and moved to the Cape where she had spent some of her earlier summers with her parents. They had both passed and she had no brother or sister, although without family, she had made a life for herself at the Cape. The winters were always hard with the bitter cold, but on those few days that she could go out, the landscapes offered her something that she felt she was able to capture: intensity and relentlessness. These were the qualities she had developed in herself.

She had been weighing the move before Joe had bought it up. The only question she had concerned was logistics. She had no doubt of her love for him nor of his for her. She was not sure if hanging on to her home was a safety net. She didn't want to feel it might keep her from being fully committed but was afraid not to have one.

"I have a proposal."

"I can't imagine what you're going to say."

"You have a house. I have a house. Let's each add our names to the deeds of the two houses. We are now a couple that has two homes."

"My life with you only gets richer and richer."

She laughed. "Don't be too sure, darling. You haven't seen my mortgage."

"The interest you show me pays for the mortgage."

"Well, as long as we're playing with words and metaphors, you're a capital kind of guy with great principles. The dividends are great, and they come more often than quarterly."

Joe was stumped. He recovered quickly. "You can always bank on me because I have no plans to cash out."

Joe called for the packers, allowing Claudia to direct what she wanted to have crated immediately for their flight to Los Angeles. She wanted her art supplies to be with her when she arrived. They discussed whether they should try and rent her place for the season and realized they would not have to make any decision for another month until after Labor Day. They could always come back and board up the place if they couldn't find a renter. Claudia was only attached to a dining room table that belonged to her parents. It was the only item she was going to bring with her when she began her new life in California. The flight from Boston to LA was smooth, and Joe smiled as he carried Claudia into his home, feeling this was really a fresh start. It was even better than the overall feeling he had with his first wife. It was better because not only did this woman love him, but he also felt secure since he no longer had to prove himself because he had been promoted to detective. He began repeating but modifying the words from "California Dreamin'" in his head. *I'll be safe and warm now that I'm in LA.*

He was looking forward and was excited to what awaited him.

CHAPTER 4

Coming Home

Zuma was welcomed back on his first day at work. They had balloons and a big chocolate cake. When he had left to go on vacation, it was with a blaze of glory having created a major drug bust and solved three murders.

Pat, his assistant, gave him a big hug.

"Happy to see you, boss. You look great. You lost some weight."

"Yes, I did a lot of walking, but mostly I'm in love and I brought her back with me from Cape Cod."

"That's great, boss. I can't wait to meet her. When you're ready to talk about work, let me know. I think you need to introduce yourself to the new recruits."

"I'm ready. Let's do it now, Pat."

"Hi everybody. My name is Joe Zuma and most of you who know me know that this is my first day back from vacation. For those who are here for the first time, you are lucky to have been selected to join this precinct. We are an unusual department, and we pride ourselves in doing good police work. We do this without hitting or threatening or beating up our suspects. Brandishing our weapons is not something you should do unless you have been notified that a suspect is dangerous or armed. So, if you come here thinking you can do things you have seen police officers doing on TV or in the Harry Bosch novels, forget it. We will train you to rely on your brains and our experiences. Bringing in a suspect, who is going to sue the city or you personally, is not what I or anyone else in this precinct wants to see. You are being paid to do police work. That is all you are allowed to do. You cannot do your laundry, run errands for your family, or eat donuts on the job. You are never to accept anything from a grateful client and certainly not from a suspect. Finally, and most importantly, all of the citizens who live here, visit here, or play here deserve our respect. Do not act on any of your preconceived notions about race, gender, dress, or cars. We have a big homeless population and we draw people from all over the globe. If any of you feel you need guidance in this area, please see my assistant, Detective Pat Vasquez. We will not hold this against you. In fact, you will look better in our eyes if you can seek this training on your own. Any questions?

"As of now, I am in charge of the precinct. Ordinarily, there should be a captain, and the district is doing a search for one. See Pat or me for any issues you have with your work. As new recruits, most of you will be assigned to the midnight shift. If that poses a hardship, please see Pat. Best of luck. Pat and I are here to help, and you are here to serve. If there are no questions, you're dismissed."

"Nice job, boss. Glad you're back. Did you miss us?"

"Believe it or not, Pat, I did miss the work. Unless there is something pressing, and since it looks like the chocolate cake is being devoured, I'd like to take the rest of the day off. I'm eager to find out how Claudia spent her first day. She's in an entirely new area, and she was going to walk on the bluffs where the homeless are located. I am a bit nervous. I don't think she's ever seen the kind of homelessness we have here."

"Sure, boss, everything can wait. I'll see you tomorrow."

"The homeless seem different here Joe. In the Cape, they suffer in the winter, but they get by in the summer. They become a bit lighter or almost happy. Here, they neither seem happy nor sad. They just seem to relish their homelessness. It's a kind of 'leave me alone and mind your own business attitude.' There's something about them that fascinates me. I've never been drawn to do portraits, but I think I want to try and capture their faces. I believe their looks and the background of the Pacific would make for intensity that I have never imagined before."

Joe was pleased that Claudia had found something so quickly upon relocating. But he was also concerned.

"Okay, you need to be careful. We've had to deal with lots of complaints about our homeless. They can be pretty aggressive. I know they will want to charge you money if you ask them to sit while you're painting. Some may even try and destroy your paints and materials. How can this be done so I will not be concerned with your safety?"

"What if I have one of those things that old people use to call their doctors? You know like when they fall down getting out of the tub and can't get up."

"I think that could do it. Let's try it out. But if it fails to get me there in time for any emergency, we have to come up with something else."

"Joe, you are most dear. And I love how we resolve our differences."

"I want to you to be my deer, but I always want you in my headlights so I can get there in time."

"I can be your deer but only if you will be my bear."

"That makes it easy. No matter how I hug you, it will be a bear hug."

CHAPTER 5

A First Day

"Pat, thanks for keeping this stuff away from me on my first day back. Wow, two murders. Fill me in."

"Sure, boss, I thought it could wait. I did some preliminaries. Here's what we know. There were two vics. One woman, twenty-eight, and the other forty-two. They were roommates."

"Tell me about the younger one. Did she have kin?"

"Her parents are both alive. They said that their daughter Lisa Beck had just returned from Europe the week before and was temporarily living with a girlfriend while looking for an apartment. She had a boyfriend whom they say she had broken up with prior to her trip. Lisa had called them on her way out to dinner with the roommate. The computer and her phone showed that ex to be a character named Jack. We found lots of professions of love and his desire to get back. Apparently, she didn't tell him where she was going. He was planning to meet her in Paris, but she went to London. She did not want to have anything to do with him."

"Why is that?"

"The parents didn't know too much. They said that Lisa just told them that Jack had hurt her with his infidelity."

"Do we know anything about her time in London? Where she stayed? What she did?"

"Text messages report theater goings, indicating she did meet someone nice on the flight over."

"Anything more on that?"

"The fellow she met on the plane, a guy named Hal, and Lisa were out to dinner three times in the week she was there."

"Sounds like it could have been more that a one-week English fling. Let's check him out. Maybe Lisa mentioned him to other girlfriends."

"Okay, boss. Neighbors say Lisa was friendly to everyone. They also report they had heard fighting with the ex a number of times. One of them said he had seen the police show up once."

"Is there a record?"

"No, she didn't want to press charges."

"And who was victim two?"

"A teacher, forty-two years old. As I said, she was Lisa's roommate."

"That does seem strange. Two roommates murdered at the same time."

"What do we know about the teacher's family?"

"Still alive in Germany. She was well-loved at the school where she taught. But, and this is a big but, boss, we found opiates in her drawers and drug paraphernalia."

"Were there enough opiates to sell or do you think it was for her personal use?"

"Couldn't tell for sure, boss. It was close. If I had to guess, it would be more towards her selling the stuff."

"Let's check with her doctor. She had to have insurance from the school. Find out when she first got the prescriptions and how often. Let's also check with her parents. She may have begun with prescribed opiates in Germany and continued use here. Need to check with her colleagues also about her usage."

"Sure, boss. Shall I start right now?"

"First, let's you and I visit Mr. 'I Will Love You Forever' Jack. After we do that, you can ask Lisa's colleagues, her parents, and her doctor whatever they might know about her usage."

CHAPTER 6

Breaking Concrete

"Joe, what kind of city have I moved into? Look at these headlines.

**'Man plows into farmers' market past
barricades and kills 4 and injures 10'
'Woman, mother of two-year-old, arrested
for scalding daughter's feet'**

When she's picked up, the mother is quoted as saying, *'I didn't want her to be walking barefoot, it's too dirty in the streets.* Joe, we have crazies at the Cape, but that kind of news is once in a blue moon. You seem to have here it every day. Hardly a day goes by without some bizarre murder or horror."

"I know, honey. I try to not let it affect me and don't want it to affect you."

"Joe, everything affects everything."

"Are you going to tell me about the butterfly flapping its wings and how that is related to the icebergs melting?"

"I can repeat that if you want."

"Do you think the butterfly caused my love for you?"

"You can't make it so concrete."

"Claudia, darling, I deal in concrete every day. My job is cracking the concrete to create a little safer space in this city. Those two headlines aren't the real bad stuff that exist out there. It's bad, but we already know who is involved."

Claudia imagined the city Joe worked in with its sidewalks and streets as having an underground city right below the one that most of its citizens use. The underground city had a concrete roof over its flat concrete surface and was where he worked and had to know if he wanted to solve crimes. She imagined a painting that could illustrate ordinary life on one surface and nefarious activities on the lower surface. The lower surface would be the Hieronymus Bosch Painting "The Harrowing of Hell" and the upper level would be something by Hopper who captured the loneliness of urban living. She filed that image in her mind and asked Joe for a moment while she quickly sketched the two-level ideas.

"My job is to find the bad ones who are not known."

He felt his reaction and explanation were too strong and sounded like he was arguing he didn't like his reaction and started to apologize. "I'm sorry, honey, it—"

"No, it's all right, Joe. I sometimes forget what you have to deal with. Maybe if you told me more about your work, I could understand."

"Claudia, you know I'll do anything you ask of me. If you want to know more about my work, I'll be happy to talk with you. But if you decide you want to hear less or even nothing, promise you'll let me know."

"I promise."

"Okay, remember the stuff I'm telling you has no known perpetrators. These are unknowns. I deal with the unsolved stuff. Here's what was on my desk this morning. When you read stuff in the papers, it involves known culprits who are going to court. I am frequently involved in the cases you read about but usually only in gathering evidence, picking up, or capturing the suspect. Claudia, no one outside the department sees this stuff. So please don't repeat what I'm going to share with you. If you read the headlines and the story, you already know that two people were shot outside the Spitfire Grill near the Santa Monica Airport. The story quoted police saying the two women were coming out of the grill and were shot up close from behind. The article ends up saying at this point there are no suspects. There are no suspects, but it's more complicated. What it doesn't say is that when we investigated, no one seemed to notice or hear the shots because a car was screeching down the street, making a lot of noise, and there may have been planes flying very close by. We have no plates on the car or even a description, and there aren't any witnesses to the shooting."

"Oh my god. what can you do?"

"Break the concrete. Start with the crime scene. We collect bullets and run ballistic tests. We have the names of the victims, so we notify next of kin. We interview them and all the other people who knew each victim. We get their computers to see if that can lead us anywhere. We ask neighbors about the kind of people these were and go from there."

"That's a lot."

"Yes, it is. And, sometimes, it leads to absolutely nowhere. I have a file on unsolved crimes on my desk now. Have a big one from last year. I'm pretty sure I know who did it, but I can't prove it. So, I keep thinking and hoping for some kind of break. We never found a murder weapon and we never even found a body. A husband just disappeared."

"Maybe he just left his family."

"That's highly improbable. He loved his daughter. Wanted out of the marriage. I think the wife did it, but we can't find the body."

"How could a wife be able to hide a body?"

"It is a big item to get rid of, but we're in a city that has lots of people out all day and all night no matter how late. There are always cars, trucks, and lots of pedestrians. Few people take notice of things going on around or in front of them."

Claudia thought she would have to imagine a different painting than the one by Hopper. There was that work by Char Wood "Big City Life" which showed citizens stepping off a curb, crossing a street. It would be perfect for the business of city life. She had always loved it because even though it was San Francisco, it seemed very much like New York.

"Joe, how could she have done it? A man's body, how do you hide that?"

"I don't know, dear. If I could answer that, the case would be solved. She was an artist like you. But she made furniture not paintings."

CHAPTER 7

From Landscapes to a Portrait

Claudia could see that the man who had agreed to pose for her was growing impatient. This was his third day and the other vagrants had been coming up and making hostile remarks to her.

She understood the loyalty that must exist among the homeless and realized that he was getting worried that he would be seen as someone who was cooperating with the enemy. She understood that he would not let her know that it was going to be his last day. She also felt that offering more money would be an empty gesture. He had to be more worried about his peers than about money or her desires. She was trying to think about having to end it before she was finished when she realized that it could be unfinished. She smiled at him and was in the process of thanking him when he jumped towards her, knocked over the painting, stomped on it, and ran off. As she picked her work up and tried to remove the dirt, she thought Joe was right. The bluffs were dangerous. But the painting didn't look damaged. And she wasn't hurt. She knew the dirt could be removed once she got back home and was relieved that none of the paint had been smudged. When she looked up, her model was not to be seen, but other homeless were watching almost gleefully. Trudging home with her easel and painting, she felt that she had given it a good shot, knowing that the work was not complete but knowing that incompleteness could be represented in the background of the man's face. In fact, she realized that the title of the work should be

"Incompleteness." When Joe got home, she recounted what had happened.

"I was not hurt and since he ran off, I was not in danger, and I didn't need any help carrying the portrait home."

"Well, I hope you have given up painting the homeless."

"I'm glad I did it. I'm not sure what I want to do now. Going back to outdoor paintings does not seem as exciting to me."

"I'm relieved you're safer. Glad you were not hurt and happy you like the work you did. I know you will find something else."

"Joe, darling, I love your confidence in me."

"It's based on admiration, respect, and truth. In case you haven't figured that out, those words begin with the letters A, R, and T."

Claudia laughed heartily and went to kiss him.

Joe hoped that this happy ending would not embolden her to more risky endeavors. That fear lasted a split second as he went on to feel the heartiness of her kiss and embrace.

CHAPTER 8

Losing the Catch

"Jack, when exactly was the last time you spoke to Lisa?"

"Well, it was a weird thing. I got a call from someone on her phone. They had apparently mistakenly exchanged phones on their way to LAX, and she was late in getting to the airport. 'That is so typically Lisa, being late and losing her phone. She would be calling me when she arrived in Europe,' the guy said. He didn't want to give me his phone number. When she called me, I discovered that she was in London. I was really pissed. I had booked a plane to Paris, had a ring, and was going to ask her to marry me in front of the Eiffel tower."

"You're quite the romantic, aren't you?"

"I loved her and realized that I didn't want to lose her."

"And what was this about an affair you had that she found out about."

"She discovered this stuff on my phone. At first, I lied but then I fessed up. I was stupid. Guess I was afraid of how serious she was."

"And what helped you lose your fear?"

"I realized that this guy she met on the plane who had taken her phone was interested, and I heard how quickly after she arrived in London that she had met another guy. I think I had a catch, but I didn't realize what I had."

"So, you were a little jealous of how quickly Lisa could go on and to meet someone else?"

"I guess I was."

"And the neighbors who reported your fighting, was that about jealousy also?"

"Yeah. Lisa was a free spirit, and I had trouble with how many friends she had and how important they were to her."

"Okay, Jack. Where were you on the night Lisa was shot?"

"OMG. Am I a suspect?"

"No, we just need to know your whereabouts."

"I was home. I went there after work, and I picked up some food to eat at home. I crashed in front of the TV."

"What time did you get home?"

"I think it must have been around nine or so.

"Can anyone verify that?"

"I'm not sure. I did open my mailbox and a neighbor walked by, but I didn't notice who it was. I think Rachel Maddow was on the tube."

"Okay, Jack, I'll keep you posted. As we learn more about the case, I may have to speak to you again. And just for the record, get rid of your Paris flight plan and don't leave the country."

"Detective, do I need a lawyer?"

"If you're innocent, why would you want one?"

"Come on, Detective, you know how innocents often end up."

"Well, if you feel that might happen to you, it's probably a good idea."

On the way back, Joe asked Pat what he thought.

"It did seem strange that he wanted a lawyer so quickly."

"I agree. We're going to have to check with everyone in the building if they remember seeing him when they left that night and also check with his work to see what time he left there."

"Right, boss. Should we do anything with the London guy? And what about the dude she met on the plane? And the other one who picked up her phone?"

"Pat, you are a man to be admired. Let's make a wall in the office with all these possible suspects. It will look like a regular TV drama. We'll put a signature at the bottom. I'll write David Wolf. Make sure all the guys in the office know it's a joke or else they'll think we've lost our marbles and hired a TV writer. I think he's great at what he does, very inventive, but the man does create creeps and, sometimes, I wonder if he also inspires creeps."

"Sometimes, boss, I get ideas from the show about methods as well as motives."

"Keep watching, Pat. We can use everything and anything in this one."

Pat knew that once a wall had been created with suspects and victims that Zuma would pull a toothpick from his left shirt pocket, place it in the corner of his mouth, and begin humming. It was always the same tune. He had been unable to recognize it but had been meaning to ask.

CHAPTER 9

A New Job

"I think I found a job."

"I didn't know you were looking for one."

"I wasn't really. I was glancing at ads, avoiding the headlines, and under A there was one: 'Artist wanted to work at private school, children ages 12-18, three afternoons a week.' It's perfect. I have the light of the wonderful sunrise, and in the evening, the sun setting over the Pacific. I get to continue to do what you said to me in Cape Cod. I remember you said, 'What is so great about California is the light. I promise you, Claudia, you will love the light.' And you were right."

"Wow. That's great. When do you start?"

"I need to interview, but the lady on the phone sounded very enthusiastic about my background and credentials."

"As they should."

"I hope you are not doing this for money. I promised you that we had enough on my salary and would have enough with a pension when I retire so you would never have to work."

"No, Joe, it's not for the money. I've been antsy ever since the stuff happened with the vagrants, and I have been looking for something. The ad really appealed to me when I saw it."

"I'm happy for you, Claudia. I'm sure you will wow them. What school is it?

"SurePaths."

That name struck a bell with Joe, but he couldn't recall where he had heard it. He didn't like that he couldn't recall where he had heard it, and he wrote the name down so he could check the files tomorrow.

CHAPTER 10

The Great Wall

Pat had put all the suspects and the victims' names and pictures on the wall.

The toothpick was in place and the humming had begun.

"This is going to be a big job, Pat. Can we eliminate anyone?"

"Yeah, boss, I told you about the London dude. His name doesn't show up as leaving Heathrow and I even checked Paris flights to LA. I think he's out."

"Let's call the Brits to see if they can verify where he was on the night of the shooting."

"Good idea, boss, I hadn't thought of that."

"Pat, you've got to watch more TV."

Zuma was staring at the names of the two victims. One name struck a bell. The SurePaths school where Claudia would be working was also resonating in his mind. The name and the school together set off the light bulb.

"Pat, the woman who was shot with Lisa was the same gal who was involved in that disappearing husband case."

"Wow, boss, if this were a Dick Wolf show, it would definitely not be a coincidence. She was the teacher that the husband was screwing right?"

"Yeah, and the wife really liked her because their daughter really loved the teacher. When the wife found out what this gal was doing with her hubby, she turned on her. I never could understand why this embittered wife could become friendly to the hubby's lover. I knew it had to be because of something about the husband but always came up empty."

"Hey, boss, maybe we can get lucky and finish the two TV shows that we have up on the board."

Fear went through Zuma's body. He did not like it that Claudia would be working at the same school where a suspect's child went. That meant the suspect in his unsolved murder case would be meeting Claudia. He was not sure why he was fearful. Maybe it was because he felt that she had outsmarted him or because she was a bit like one of those Dick Wolf's creepy characters. Fear, for Zuma, was a rare occurrence. He had better talk to Claudia about it. When Zuma realized that the woman who had been with Lisa was the suspect in the disappearing husband case, he stopped humming. Pat hadn't noticed, and now it was too late to ask for the name of the song.

CHAPTER 11

Eliminating and Adding

"That's a huge rogues gallery, Pat." The toothpick was out, and the humming had started.

"Yeah, boss, but a lot of them are unlikely, and I think we can start eliminating."

"Go ahead and eliminate."

"The London guy never left. I checked all airlines from the day Lisa landed to the day she was killed, and no airline leaving London had his name. I also checked arrivals in LAX for the same period and struck out. That's one down."

"Pat, we need to stretch our search for information a bit wider. First, I'd like you to add the name of that woman from the unsolved disappearance of her husband. Second, can we check on the other victim, Hope, the teacher at SurePaths. I'd like you to run all the phone calls she's made and received in the past month. Let's speak to her neighbors as to what they might have noticed that made them suspicious. Who else is up on our board?"

"There are the two other guys who Lisa met. The one whom she exchanged phones with and the one she met on the plane going to London. You already interviewed the ex-boyfriend, and when I checked with all the neighbors one did see him at his mailbox. She said hello but he ignored her."

"Did she give you a time?"

"Yeah, she was pretty sure it was seven o'clock since she was on her way to meet a friend for dinner."

"Let's keep Mr. Eiffel Tower on our board. He was not seen after the neighbor saw him. And Rachel Maddow could be his fake news story. Remember Maddow is on at six and nine, our time. So immediate stuff is speaking with London air flight guy and phone exchange guy."

"I'm on it. Boss, what is the name of the tune you were humming when you're thinking?"

It's a song by Bob Dylan. Why don't you look up the tunes he wrote and make a guess?"

CHAPTER 12

A Child

"We're very pleased that you can join our faculty, Ms. Berlin. Is there anything we can do to help you get started? We will, of course, introduce you to each of the classes you will be meeting. And you can decide what sort of artwork you will want them to engage in."

"Please call me, Claudia. I like the informality that exists in California. It's so much more inviting than the formality that we cultivate back East. I think it will be better if I offer them some choices. Drawing in pencil or pen? Watercolors? I think I will offer oil paintings to the older children."

"You could either pick up supplies or you can call and have them delivered. We can pay the store directly since we have an account there. All the kids are pretty well adjusted. I do want to alert you to one of the older children. Her name is Lucy. She lost her dad a year ago and now she lost her favorite teacher. She seems depressed and may not be able to perform to expectations you have."

"I will be gentle and let her be if that's what she wants."

"Thank you. Her mom is very concerned, and she may want to speak to you."

"I'll be happy to speak with her."

"A heads up about her also. She is a strong-willed person. Don't be surprised if she tries to tell you what kind of artwork she would want her daughter to do."

"Oh, is she an artist?"
"Yes. She makes furniture."

Joe become very quiet after Claudia told him about the school and that she would be working with the furniture maker's daughter.

"I'm not happy about this. That woman is trouble. I don't think you're in danger, but it's not as if I can just ignore that you may be talking to a murder suspect of ours."

"Joe, I promise you I will not take her to lunch or visit her studio. The only thing I will do is talk with her about her daughter. I will not bring you up or inquire about her deceased husband."

"I don't have a problem with you, Claudia dear. I trust you. I don't trust that child's mother. She is an excellent liar, wily, cagy, and can't be trusted."

CHAPTER 13

Stolen Art

"Joe, can you please come home. I just got back from teaching and my painting is gone."

"Which one?"

"The one with the homeless guy."

"Are you okay?"

"Yes, nothing else seems to be stolen. None of the other art works. The house is not messed up."

Claudia was not the kind of woman who would ask for help unless needed. He rushed home, telling Pat there was a robbery at home.

"Do you want me to come with you?"

"No, Pat. I think I can be more calming to Claudia if we don't make it a crime scene right away."

Claudia was right. Nothing was messy. The robber or robbers seemed to know exactly what they wanted. The painting had been resting on an easel, so it was easy to find it and leave. Joe checked to see if the locks had been jimmied or the windows broken. He found the window that was slightly ajar.

"Honey, it looks like you forgot to make sure to lock the windows and put on the alarm?"

"I'm sorry. I forget I'm not living at the Cape anymore."

Joe wondered what the robber would have done if the alarm had been set. He registered that if only a single item had been stolen, it must have been important, and important enough to risk getting caught. He also realized that Claudia must have been under surveillance, as the robber knew the house was empty. The robber knew that Claudia did the painting, where she lived, and now had a painting that could not be easily shown by its new owner. He was puzzled trying to imagine what was so important about having a painting that you couldn't show or sell?

CHAPTER 14

A Wooden Proposal

"Ms. Berlin, thank you for meeting with me. The school and I felt it was important that I speak with you about my child. My daughter has lost her father in the past year and now her favorite teacher has been murdered."

"I have been told about those two incidents. They are catastrophic for anyone, especially for a child. What would you like to let me know?"

"Lucy, and maybe it was because of her teacher, had become quite interested in my work. She started hanging around in my studio. I don't know if you know it, but I make custom furniture. I began to let her help me. I never gave her big tools or large pieces of wood but small sanders and softer wood that she could carve with a knife. She was able to sand and polish the things she made, and she really liked doing it. It was the first time since her dad disappeared that I saw her old spark. I was wondering if you would allow her to continue this in your art class?"

"I'd love to, but I have to check with the school administration first. They might not be so open to having knives in the classroom. And if they do approve, I would have to offer it as an option to all members of the class. I'm sure all the boys would jump on it."

"I can show the principal how safe the sanders and the knives would be. Perhaps you could help the children understand safety and how they are never to brandish or wave it in the air."

"It's probably a good thing and it does fit in with telling them, despite how much they would enjoy it, about the dangers of splashing paint on others."

"If the school accepts my plan, I will be happy to supply all the tools and the wood."

"That would probably help in convincing them since it won't cost them a penny."

"Would you be willing to come with me when I speak to the head honcho so he knows you support it and you can talk about safety?"

Claudia's instincts were to say yes. She liked the idea of offering more options in her class and knew more boys would want to be in it if woodworking was an option. She also felt that she did not want Joe to feel that she was cooperating fully with this woman. She recalled Joe's emphatic "I don't trust her."

"I think you should go on your own, and if the school board or whoever wants to speak with me, I guarantee you that I will support your proposal."

"Thank you so much, Ms. Berlin. I appreciate that as an artist you are helping another artist. I welcome a visit from you to my studio. I just need a head's up as I work pretty much every day."

Joe was not at all pleased to hear that his suspect had spent time with Claudia and had invited her to the studio.

"Joe, there's a hurt, damaged child involved here. I'm doing this for the child. I don't have to be involved with the mother."

"I know you feel that way now. But she is a manipulator, a liar, and a suspect to a murder. You have got to tell me about any and all contacts you have with her."

"I will, Joe. Remember you said you trust me."

"And remember I said I love you."

"Joe, sweetheart, you are the apple of my eye."

"Happy you don't think that I'm a bad seed."

"Joe, everything is going to be just peachy."

"I think we better stop right now. This is going to turn into a compote."

"Yes, we do need to pare it down."

"Just prune your contacts with her."

They started giggling and both of them forgot about the liar and murder suspect.

CHAPTER 15

The Minor Theft

"Pat, it was only one of her paintings. Nothing else was touched. Why do you think it was only one?"

"Well, the painting was about that homeless guy. Maybe he didn't want anyone to have it or see it. Maybe he was worried that someone he knew would see he was homeless and come after him, like his family, that he wanted nothing to do with."

"Maybe? Or maybe, Pat, someone who knew this guy wanted it for some other reason. Let's think like Dick Wolf. The more obvious thief would be the hobo. Why would someone else not want that picture to be in the public eye?"

"I like that idea, boss."

"Before we start doing anything about who might that be, let's keep a lookout for the guy. They usually come back to their begging haunts. He may return."

"Okay, boss. Write the TV drama."

"The homeless guy is selling drugs. His dealer doesn't want any attention given to him beyond the people who buy from him."

"I like that, boss."

"Since there may be a dealer involved, let's start asking our snitches on the bluff if they ever saw Claudia's model with anyone who looked like he was not homeless."

"Okay, but if he was getting drugs from this guy, it would probably not be in daylight on the bluffs."

"You're right, Pat. If that doesn't turn up anything, let's find who among those guys were close to Claudia's model. We will pay for information. There's loyalty among thieves and the homeless but when there is money, loyalty can fade."

"Boss, I looked up some of the Dylan songs."

"'Don't Think Twice' would not be you, but the other one, 'Like a Rolling Stone,' was not you either."

"Keep trying, Pat."

CHAPTER 16

A Well-Meaning Prescription

"Pat, we've got a lot going here. A stolen painting, a theory of drugs or drug dealing, two vics, one with drug paraphernalia and lots of suspects. Do you have anything about the teacher's drug use?"

"Her parents said that Hope had broken one knee and two hips in a skiing accident. That was about six years ago, and that is when she started opiate usage. They are pretty careful in Germany, but we know the stuff can easily become addicting. She told her doctor that while she was in the US she still needed the stuff. That was two years ago. He was reluctant, but she said it was the only way she could stand up for the long day in front of her class. When he suggested that she go on leave or take sick leave, she balked and said the school would get mad because she hadn't told them about her condition beforehand."

"How often did he prescribe?"

"He said he was careful but that prescriptions can easily be forged."

"Pat, I think we have an addict. Or I should say it looks like an addict was shot. That throws a whole new light on possible motives at least about the teacher. What did you pick up from her fellow teachers?"

"She loved her kids. They could see mood swings. If she came into school with low energy, by ten a.m. at a break, they could see shifts in her mood."

"That confirms addictive behavior. She takes an opiate, and now she can conquer the world and love the kids."

"Okay, boss. Let's go to the drawing board."

"We start out with two vics, one an addict the other a roommate with no known vices. The one without known vices has three men, each of whom could be jealous enough to murder."

"The more likely one to be the guy who probably goes around singing, 'Some Enchanted Evening.'"

"Boss, I don't know that one. Must be way before my time. I think we can eliminate the London English one-week fling."

"Okay, but also put her parents up on the board. We need to find out from them if Lisa had ever mentioned the opiate usage to them. If they knew about the opiate usage, I'm sure they would have been very upset and may have gone to the school. We are going to have to visit the principal."

"Boss, this is getting complicated. We're going to need a bigger board."

"Yes, we are. We have to add a break-in and a stolen painting. I'm sure you know me well enough to know that I believe that all these matters are related." Zuma started humming.

"I sure do, boss. And I've been around you long enough to know that you're crazy thinking often turns out to be right. Boss, is the name of that tune you always hum when you're looking at our board 'Blowin in the Wind?'"

"You got it. I knew you would."

CHAPTER 17

Lucy into the Wood

"Lucy, those are lovely figures. Did you have anyone in mind when you carved them?"

"My daddy, my mommy, and my teacher."

"Do you want to take them home now to show Mommy or would you be able to wait until we put on our Christmas show and have all the school see your work?"

"I'll take them home to show Mommy, and then I can bring them back."

"Good idea. Let me wrap them up for you so they won't break, and you can surprise your mom."

"Claudia, thank you for sending Lucy's work with her. She told me you wanted them back for your Christmas show and sale. I am really grateful for all you are doing for her. I would like to contribute a furniture piece to the show. I'll pay for its delivery."

"That's very generous of you. I think you should check with the school when they would be able to receive it. We fill the whole auditorium with donations."

Claudia thought of telling her that she also was going to donate something but, again, Joe's words reverberated inside her head.

"Claudia, I would like to ask you something."

Claudia tensed. Was manipulation on the way?

"When Hope was alive, she had planned to take Lucy on some weekend trips. She was going to introduce Lucy to skiing, and I think they were also going to do whale watching."

"Did Lucy get to do those things?"

"No. Here is what happened. Even when Lucy told me about the trips, I felt she wasn't that excited. I don't know if it was mother's intuition or not, but I asked her if there was some reason that she might not want to go, and she said these exact words. 'Hope has bloodshot eyes every morning. She doesn't seem happy.'

"I wondered what was going on, thinking she might be struggling with a relationship. I decided to go to school and speak with her. When I made my appointment, I told Hope that as much as I felt that Lucy loves her, she was hesitant to go away with her.

"'Did Lucy tell you why?'

"'No, but I wondered if you might know why that would be true?'

"'I have been under lots of stress. I don't know if you know this, but I had two hip replacements and a knee injury a while back. The doctor is trying to figure out a new drug for me to help with my pain since the old ones don't seem to work anymore. It's taken quite a while for us to figure out what works.'

"Claudia, that didn't sound right to me. I actually thought she was lying and must be showing up at school half drugged. I suggested she take some time off from teaching and that the school would understand. She said she did not want to take time off but was confident that her doctor would soon figure it out. I left there with a bad feeling, but I was not going to let Lucy go on any trips with her. I debated talking to the school but shelved that. I was going to give her the benefit of the doubt and wait and see. When she was murdered, I didn't have to do anything. I figured that maybe one of the reasons she got shot had to do with drugs. This is my question for you. Would you consider the possibility of inviting Lucy for a weekend?"

Claudia thought how easy it would be to say yes if she hadn't known anything about this woman. She seemed kind and concerned with a sense of strong devotion to her child. And Claudia had developed a strong feeling of affection for Lucy.

"I really don't know. I have a husband and I would have to check with him. Our time is pretty tight as he and I work on weekends, but I will ask and get back to you. If we can, it will probably be after Christmas."

"Oh, that would be fine. There is no rush. Lucy hasn't brought it up. Bring your husband to our Christmas sale so Lucy and I can meet him."

Claudia shuddered. Her brows began to knit and she grimaced as she imagined the scene of Joe and her meeting with the gloom that would arise the moment Sonia would realize that Claudia was married to the detective who had investigated her for murder. Claudia felt like she was being lured into something. She knew Joe would say absolutely no to any weekends with Lucy, but he could not say no to the Christmas event. And even if he did say no, she would ask him to come with her. Meeting the man who had investigated her husband's disappearance and possible murder might put an end to the luring and manipulation.

CHAPTER 18

Paintings in Shangri-La

"One of our snitches said that Carl, the name of the model that Claudia painted, did not want his family to know where he was and that could have been a reason for his stealing the painting. He also said that Carl was selling to others on the beach, including the runners and walkers. Apparently, he did not frighten the straights. That must have been what Claudia saw in his face, some form of kindness."

"She did see something that she wanted to capture, and where did our snitch think that Mr. Kindness got his supply?"

"He wasn't sure, but he used to see Carl hanging out in front of the Shangri-La Hotel, the one on Ocean Avenue."

"I know it, Pat. Claudia loves it because it has this wonderful op art deco design. She's also fascinated by its history. Supposedly, it has something to do with the Nazis. We were told that one of Hitler's architects designed the hotel in 1940. I did a search, and the story about Hitler is utter nonsense. The hotel was used for intelligence meetings and by our troops during WW II. I go there because the food is good, and you can see the sunsets if you get the right table. The maître de knows us and has asked Claudia to put some of her paintings there. They get tourists and I suggested to her that a Cape Cod visitor to our fair city might be touched to see his home in Santa Monica."

"Are her paintings there?"

"No. She's thinking about it. Let's post someone to be there every day, about an hour before sunset. That's when I think Carl might have finished examining his backpack to see if it needs refilling. Mr. Kindness can't show up in the morning without having dope or drugs for his clients. And if we can get a picture of the person he's meeting, we can run it through the files. But I don't want to do anything until we know who this guy is and how he might fit in to a bigger ring of dealers."

"Boss, could I join you and Claudia at the Shangri-La for a drink?"

"Of course, Pat. We can even make it a dinner that I shall be happy to buy for you, but you can't buy any of her works."

"Why not, boss?"

"Because I'm hoping they're way out of your price range."

CHAPTER 19

Paintings and a Party

"Boss, the guy we saw and took a picture of turned up squeaky clean. I followed him into the bar and after he had a drink and left, I managed to get his name from the bartender when I showed him my badge. He commented that the guy was a generous tipper and always came in alone."

"What else did you find out?"

"He has a printing business and he also does banners and trophies for awards. I went to his shop and there's lots of stuff for kids' games and school contests. Name is Guy Roy."

"Good work, Pat. Let's find out if he's interested in paintings."

"You mean Claudia's?"

"Yeah, but not her landscapes. I'm going to ask Claudia to do a sketch of the homeless man she had done earlier. She can do it in charcoal. She's good at that, and I think she can get it done quickly. We can put it up along with her landscapes in the hotel and see if Mr. Roy wants to purchase it. We need to ask the bartender to let us know if he does as he may want to pay cash and there will be no receipt."

"Big favor, honey. From your memory, can you do a charcoal sketch of the homeless man you painted?"

"Sure, Joe. When do you need it by?"

"Whenever you finish it will be fine. I'd like you to pick out two more paintings of yours so that it will be less conspicuous, and it can be advertised as the work of a local resident. We will put all three at the Shangri-La."

"And I would like you to come with me to the Christmas fundraising party at my school. I need to tell you—"

"I will do that for you."

"I didn't finish. Your suspect is going to be there. I told her I have a husband and she is looking forward to meeting you."

Zuma paused for a moment and took a deep breath.

"Claudia, darling, I'm a great believer in the value of surprises. I look forward to seeing the look on her face. I also like the idea that she learns that we are a couple. She might become less involved and more wary and ask you less about Lucy once she knows the two of us are together."

"But you have got to be pleasant at this party, Joe. I don't want anything that seems like an interrogation."

"Of course, I assume the furniture maker when she sees me will become as smooth as her highly polished furniture and as hard as her wood."

Zuma began thinking about another way to find out more about Guy Roy.

"Joe, I know your wheels are spinning because I hear your humming. I guess something is 'blowin in the wind?'"

"You're right, honey. Can I increase my request for two of those charcoal paintings that I asked you for?"

CHAPTER 20

Parents of the Victim

"Boss, we can speak to her parents directly. They're still in town. They have been waiting to clear out Hope's apartment."

"That will save the taxpayers' money. Let's not drag them down to the station, Pat. Ask them where they are staying and tell them we have a few questions."

"Mr. and Mrs. Schnable, thanks for meeting with us. You have our heartfelt condolences about the loss you have suffered."

"Your country is described in Germany as unsafe, and we are now convinced it is true. In our country, teachers are a well-respected profession and are rarely murdered. In your country, teachers get shot all the time. Why would someone want to murder our daughter?"

Joe thought of the camps with all the respected professionals, including teachers, being marched to the gas chambers but let their challenge pass.

"I am hopeful that we can capture the person or persons who killed your daughter and bring them to justice. At this point, I can't tell you anything because it is an ongoing case. We do have some questions about Hope."

"We will help you in any way we can."

"After your daughter had the terrible accident breaking her hips and a knee, she was given some drugs. Did you know that?"

"Yes, of course. She was in excruciating pain, and the doctor who prescribed them said it was better for her healing if she could move around and so the drugs allowed her to move and recover more rapidly."

"And did you feel that at any time that Hope was becoming addicted to the drugs that were prescribed. That is not such an uncommon thing."

There was a long pause before Mrs. Schnable answered.

"We were worried. The doctor wanted her to cut back after about eight months, but Hope said she needed to continue. We talked to her about her having a possible addiction, but she dismissed it. When she left for America, we were very worried because she had managed to get her doctor in the States to take on the same medical dosage. Hope said she needed to be sure that she could stand up for her teaching assignment. We were very proud of her when we found out that the school that hired her had a great reputation for turning out creative students."

"And did Hope ever say anything or act in such a way that you felt she was addicted."

"On her two visits to us, she did sleep a lot and seemed moody, but we assumed it was jet lag. She only stayed for three days and jet lag lasts longer than that."

"Mr. and Mrs. Schnable, is there anything else you can tell us that you think is important?"

"We did speak to the principal about Hope, and we asked him about the kind of teacher she was and about her relationship to kids. He was very forthcoming in his praises of Hope. When I asked him if he was ever suspicious of drug usage or anything that looked like addictive behavior, he was vague."

"What did he say, Mr. Schnable?"

"He said they had concerns about how close she had gotten to some kids and that she was buying gifts or presents for some kids but not for others. She wasn't doing this in her classroom but after classes when a few students hung around. When we asked her about the gifts she was giving, she said it was only candy for the students who were working extra hard in her class. We were okay with that, but a parent called and said the candy their son was using had coke in it. The principal said he was about to call Hope in, but she got shot. We asked about what he did about the other kids who may have been getting the candy, but the principal was vague again, saying they were investigating that."

"Mr. and Mrs. Schnable, thank you. The two of you have been most helpful. I'll need the name and the phone number of the doctor you consulted in Germany. Can you provide that to us?"

"Yes, of course. And thank you, Detective. I'm glad we could tell someone about this. Maybe some children can be saved."

CHAPTER 21

A Principal with Few Principles

"Mr. Tapper, what did you do once you found out that at least one child had been given candy containing drugs?"

"I'm sure, Detective Zuma, you realize that I had to be very careful. If the papers got hold of this, we would have a massive drop in enrollments and a number of lawsuits."

"Yes, we realize that, but what did you do?"

"I want you to promise me that what I am going to tell you is off the record and in strict confidence. If you can't, I will have to call in a lawyer."

"Can't do that. I can, if you don't want to talk more, bring you down to the station for an interview. You can bring your lawyer."

"I'm going to have to take a chance with you, Detective. I know your wife teaches here, and I'm sure you do not want to see the school go down. It's a school that has an international reputation and its collapse would be a huge loss to Santa Monica. Before I had the chance to do anything, my nightmare came true. I got a call from a very irate and rageful parent who said he was going to the newspapers and would file a lawsuit against the school and me personally. I tried to calm him down and told him I wanted to fix things for him and his child in case the boy had been using and might have had a problem with addiction. I begged him to hold off on the newspaper and lawsuits until we knew more and to accept a peace offering."

"You mean you bought him off."

"I'm embarrassed to say so, Detective Zuma, but I cancelled his fees for this year and the next two school years. That's a seventy-five-thousand-dollar loss for us."

"Was that enough to keep him quiet?"

"So far, it looks so. He is coming in to sign a contract to not report anything in exchange for free tuition."

"That's illegal. He is required by law to report drug use by his child. And so are you."

"Well, I'm hoping he doesn't know that. I have to protect our school."

"And your ass, Mr. Tapper. Unfortunately, you are violating the law also."

"Can you just please wait till after our fundraiser before you do anything to me? It's just a week away, and it might give us a big enough cushion to withstand a lawsuit. If I am judged guilty, I can serve my sentence knowing that at least the school survived."

"Expect a visit after your fundraiser. Don't leave town, and I'll be checking every day to see that you are at the school."

CHAPTER 22

A Celebration

"Joe, this is wonderful. A guy from Provincetown paid $24,000 for the two landscapes and $300 for the homeless drawing. He asked if I lived there or here, and when the barkeep told him I lived here he wanted my number, but the barkeep got his and he said to make sure I call him. Joe, you were right, a tourist gets nostalgic for his home at a distance from his home."

"$24,300 smackeroos. Holy mackerel," said Pat.

"No, Pat, it was a whale of a sale," said Zuma.

Claudia picked up the fish idea right away.

"And I have more minnows to show him."

"And you never have to sell your sole."

Pat suddenly felt he was listening to a foreign language.

"You're right, I could just stay here and paint on my perch."

"And just for the halibut you can wait till you want to cast off for more cod."

They giggled and giggled, and Pat understand he was witnessing pillow humor.

"So, the piece that we thought would lure our thief has now been shipped to the Cape. Mr. Hobo has hitched a ride cross-country."

"Joe, I'm going to call the buyer right now and tell him that I will take pictures of a number of paintings that I think are the best ones and, if he is interested, I can bring them back to the Cape when we go there next summer, no obligation expected."

"That's wonderful, darling. But could you also do another charcoal to hang here? I think that we might still be able to find the local who feels the need to own it. And if you can put it in with two more of your landscape paintings, that would be good."

"I can do that. So, you want one for this hotel and another one for our fundraiser? I think I better start numbering them."

"Put a number 4 on the one for the fundraiser. That might create panic in our thief if he realizes he hasn't got all of them. It won't hurt the fundraising as he will buy the one you place there. The school will get its money, and it might lead us to the thief. It's as good an idea as was in the movie, *To Catch a Thief*."

"Okay, I can have that ready in time for the fundraiser."

"I better get our house lined up for our Cape Cod holiday and get ready for more whoppers."

Joe was disappointed that the charcoal sketch had been purchased by an out-of-state character but was pleased that Claudia had sold two of her major pieces and would be able to draw another one in time for the fundraiser. The fundraiser made him think of the paintings, the suspect searching for paintings of Mr. Hobo, Mr. Hobo himself, and the cross-country flights of the paintings. The innocent effort to paint had developed into a mess involving robbery, possible drugs, and probably more. He was relieved that the champagne arrived at that moment.

"Let's toast and then order. Pat, I expect you to order the best steak in the house."

"To our talented CCC."

"Boss, what's that?"

"Creative Cultured Claudia."

CHAPTER 23

The Fundraiser

Immediately upon entering, Joe spotted the two massive chests. They were placed parallel to each other and everyone who entered had to walk past them. The price was $16,000 apiece or $30,000 for the two. He had to admit they were gorgeous, a featured varnish that permitted the redwood grains to be seen and allowed a reflection of the onlooker. He saw Sonia who did notice him as she walked directly towards Claudia. When she was a few feet away, she stopped abruptly as she recognized the man who had been the investigator in her husband's disappearance. She recovered very quickly, but Joe spotted the fluttering in her eyes and the deep inhalation of breath. Claudia also saw it and quickly introduced Joe.

"This is my husband, Sonia, Detective Joe Zuma. Joe, this is Sonia."

Joe knew in advance that he was not going to indicate prior contact and waited for Sonia's response. She politely said her "hello and glad to meet you" and Joe responded in kind.

"Your furniture pieces look lovely. Everyone is going to see your work. I'm sure that you will get more potential buyers if the school is able to sell them."

"I hope so, and I love your scapes and the hobo is very touching. Did you do that here?"

"Yes, as a matter of fact. He moved me. He seemed different from the others. His face had a forward outward look, which made him appear to me as hopeful."

"I think you have captured him."

A parent tapped Sonia on the shoulder. "We just bought your two pieces. We have a summerhouse on Vancouver Island. Do you think you can do them a bit smaller and in a lighter wood? We'd be happy to give you an advance."

Sonia said her excuse-me to Joe and Claudia and walked a few feet away with the couple.

"I prefer to wait for any deposit until you see what I come up with. I'll provide you with samples of the wood and a sketch of what it would look like and you can decide if you like it. Would you be willing to come to my studio when I have it ready for you? If you do decide to commission me, I'll want half of the money at that time and the remainder when it is ready. There will be no charge for the sketch or for the samples. The charges for shipping will be your responsibility."

"Of course. We would be happy to visit your studio."

Joe leaned over and whispered. "I told you she is strong."

"She sure is. I can't negotiate the way she does."

"You don't have to, Claudia. I don't think I would like it if you were that businesslike with your art. Let's go see if you have any buyers for your work."

As they waded through the crowd, Joe felt it had been a standoff. Whatever Sonia felt was not available to his eye. He was sure that she registered that he was still around and closer than she had thought or liked.

"Look, one of my paintings and the hobo has been purchased."

"That's terrific, and you don't have to negotiate."

Joe was curious about whether there had been two buyers or one but the name of the person who purchased the hobo painting was what he was determined to get. He would have to wait till the wine tasting and serving of hors d oeuvres were completed and until the announcements had been made.

Mr. Tapper got on the mike. "Ladies and gentlemen. We have raised $672,000 for our school. We wish to thank all the artists and everyone else who made this possible. The food was donated by Fig Restaurant and Shutters at the Beach, wines were from The Duck Blind and Broadway Wine and Spirits. Those delicious homemade cakes and cookies were made by our wonderful parents. It was truly a community effort. Let's clap our hands in celebration of ourselves. If you purchased anything and want to pick it up now, line up to my right so we can bring it to you. If you would like to have it delivered, line up to my left and we will arrange for that. There will be no charge for local deliveries."

Joe waited for Claudia's purchases to be delivered. A man had purchased both of her landscapes. He was shocked when he saw to whom the hobo painting was delivered. It was a woman.

CHAPTER 24

Long Distance Deliveries

"That long-distance call to the doc in Germany paid off big time, boss. He said that he had given a prescription for Hope to use in the US. I asked if he had any other thoughts about Hope or the Schnables. He told me that about a month after Hope left that they called and said they needed a prescription for themselves. They were insistent about opiates, saying that Hope had occasionally let them use some of hers when they were in pain. They emphasized how that had worked for them. He wasn't sure if the husband had had hip surgery but did recall that the wife had surgery on her knees."

"So far, Pat, nothing unusual."

"So far, but the story ain't over. They both got their regular prescriptions and wanted to increase the dosage. As they were older, the doc thought they would probably die from old age before they would die from an overdose. So, he kept prescribing."

"Still nothing unusual."

"Okay, boss, but how about this. I checked with the three post offices closest to where they lived and bingo. In each of them, the clerk I spoke with remembered the Schnables. The clerks were hesitant at first, but when we told them what had happened to their daughter, they came around and told us that the parents came every third week to ship something to their daughter in America. The guys in the post office said shipping drugs out of Germany is very difficult. You have to fill out a large number of forms and be interviewed. But they persevered. The Schnables said it was their daughter's favorite cookies and that she couldn't get anything like that in America. All the clerks suspected that it might have had drugs, but the Schnables had the forms they had completed. They showed up to each different post office once every three weeks."

"Got it. Her favorite cookie is an opiate cookie. She could get opiates illegally in America, but much cheaper from Germany and much safer when your parents are the supplier."

"Did you find the address to where it was shipped?"

"I did, boss. This took some time as they had gone back and checked their records. But when I called again, each of the three post offices confirmed they were shipped to a PO Box in Santa Monica. I got the number."

"Great work, Pat. Get over there and see if there is a package that hasn't been picked up yet.

If there is, we can show it to the Schnables who might enjoy munching on their homemade cookies."

CHAPTER 25

A Quick Trip

"Joe, I've been thinking about what I said to Sonia."

"Me too. Maybe it's the same thing but let me go first. Claudia, I would be most honored, and I would consider myself the luckiest man in the world if you would consider marrying me."

"Joe, I was thinking the same thing. I didn't like pretending to Sonia or anyone else we were married, and of course, I say yes. Yes, a thousand times."

"I know this is crazy, but do you think we could do it on a weekend at the Cape, the place we met?"

"That's perfect. I know a nice man who is a judge and his wife knows my art. I'm sure he would be willing to do it. They will probably volunteer their house or else we can do it in the restaurant where I gave you my drawing. I'll call him right now and find out if he has any time in the next few weekends. His name is Saul Billings and his wife is Sarah. She bought a painting of herself standing at the water's edge in Truro with a school of dolphins swimming behind her. They are a wonderful couple."

"They sound great."

"Would you like to ask your boys? They could be best men. I'd like to ask the gallery owner, Lenny Gold, to give me away. He knows me the longest. We can take them all out to dinner after our ceremony. I know Saul will regale us with his stories of his time on the bench."

I'll call my boys the moment you find out when the judge is available. They will be ecstatic."

CHAPTER 26

Duplicates Matter

"Before you leave with your painting, Mrs. Roy, I'd like to ask you a few questions. I'm Detective Joe Zuma from the Santa Monica Police Department and this is my colleague, Pat Vasquez."

"Oh, I saw the security outside but didn't think we needed it inside the school. I had never seen it before inside the school. Glad if I can be of help."

"I was interested in knowing why you purchased that particular painting."

"My husband and I collect art. We are interested in art. What other possible reasons might I have for purchasing the piece?"

"I didn't say there were others."

"I did have another reason for this particular purchase."

"Please go on."

"I had seen the painting in my husband's apartment."

"Oh, you're not married?"

"Incorrect. We are married, Detective. We each have separate condos in the same building. I am a photographer and need to have lots of quiet time and a big space to work. I had stopped in his condo to deliver some mail that had been delivered incorrectly to my mailbox in our building. At his condo, I saw a painting similar to the one at the school sale. I thought I could either make a good investment, as he is pretty sharp when it comes to value in art, or I could make him jealous by owning my own. It seemed to me that I couldn't lose, and I was looking forward to his finding out that I had done it."

"So, you were here today not because your husband asked you?"

"Absolutely not. I was surprised that he wasn't here. But I also showed up because I know the school. I volunteer to teach a once-a-week class in photography."

"And was there something about the painting itself that appealed to you aside from your husband owning a copy?"

"Yes, I know the bluffs, and I was an art major at UCLA and since I photograph people, the painting captured my eye. When we were married, we would spend a fair amount of time collecting art. We would even travel abroad to collect."

"So, your decision to purchase that painting was based on your judgment of the art."

"In part, yes. It had some other appeal to me. I know the bluffs, I know the homeless problem on the bluffs, and it seemed that the painter had captured something about the bum, I mean homeless person, that made me feel sympathetic. It is a good, well-done piece of art."

"And there were no other works that appealed to you?"

"There were. I loved the furniture, but those pieces are out of my league, pricewise. Plus, they are way too big for my condo."

"Thank you, Mrs. Roy. I may have to call you again."

"Tell me, Detective, why all the fuss about this sketch?"

"It's also like yours, an interesting story, but unfortunately, I can't give you any details. However, we think your purchase may have something to do with a robbery we are investigating."

"I hope I didn't purchase a stolen work of art. I wouldn't want to give it back. I like it a lot. I'm sure it's worth more than I paid for it."

"No, Mrs. Roy, I can guarantee that your purchase is safe. It was not stolen."

"Well, I hope my husband's work was stolen. That would make me feel good. Goodbye, Detective. I hope you catch the robber and recover the lost painting."

"Pat, that yarn sounded so smooth and well-rehearsed."

"I agree, boss."

"Follow her and see where she delivers it. We know where Mr. Roy lives. If she goes to his place, call me and we can drop in to see how they will explain their desire to own two similar paintings."

"Boss, would you say to me as you might say to Claudia, she has given us great bait and we may have caught a whopper?"

Zuma smiled and thought how clever it was that Pat had remembered their repartee.

"Yes, I would, Pat. She is really helping us to cast a wide net."

CHAPTER 27

Cookies

"Mr. and Mrs. Schnable, thanks for seeing us again. We were able to get into Hope's post office box after we showed the clerk her death certificate. We opened it in front of him so there would be a witness. And it is just as you said, a box of what definitely looks like homemade cookies. We were tempted but thought better of it and thought you might like to have them."

They both froze but the wife recovered quickly.

"Well, the two of you have to sit down while I put them on a plate in the kitchen and make some coffee, so we can all enjoy them."

Zuma and Pat had prepared for what they thought might be the Schnables' responses but were caught off guard by the wife's offer. Would she dare offer them cookies that had an opiate? They heard the loud "Oi Gott im Himmel" from the kitchen.

The three of them rushed in to see Mrs. Schnable with her hands in the sink trying to retrieve some of the cookies.

"I was soaking my dishes and after I put the cookies on the plate, it slipped, and they all fell in. We can't eat these cookies with soap in them."

Zuma smiled. He admired the quick and particular way that the wife had tried to dump the evidence of opiates, but they had prepared for this."

"No problem, Mrs. Schnable! We decided to remove a few of them from the package and they are being examined right now for ingredients. Maybe you will be able to tell us the recipe before we hear from the lab."

"Sit down, Detectives, and let us explain."

"Before you do that, I need to warn you that everything you say now may be used against you in a court t of law. You also have the right to call a lawyer and have him or her present if you still want to answer, and of course you can remain silent."

Mr. Schnable spoke. "We know our rights, Detective. We have those American murder mystery series on German TV speaking to their suspects."

"Would you like to speak now?"

Both murmured yes and she began.

"After we sent Hope a few packages, she began sending us money. We were surprised as she had told us how expensive things were in America, but we were pleased to receive funds. We both are on pensions and even though our health plans are good, we live very frugally. Hope's money made a difference. We were free from, as you say in English, counting pennies. We thought she might be selling it, but that would be like so many others in the world and in your country, especially. When we came here after she was killed and found out that there was a possibility that she had been giving it to the children so they could be sellers or to the parents of the children, we were horrified. Horrified that we had contributed to our own daughter's death."

"I'm going to take you down to the precinct and book you on violating the laws regarding the shipping of opiates into this country. You will have to give up your passports and you are not to leave the country. You will probably have to face charges of mailing drugs into the US without a license. I don't fully know the law on this, so I'm not sure what other charges you might face. You may want to get a lawyer."

"Detective, we are old. We have lost our daughter. Anything that is done to us can't be so terrible. We will cooperate with you and anyone else in trying to catch the person who murdered our child. Hopefully, now that we have been caught, there are no more drugs going into the children's hands. We can't afford a lawyer but feel we don't need one. We admit our guilt. We are responsible."

Zuma recognized survivor's guilt. He knew it well from his wife's murder. But he also believed their words about responsibility were heartfelt.

"We'll drive you in, and I'll try to make sure you are not going to be held for more than one night. I'll have to speak to my boss and the DA about your cooperative behavior and ask them not to have you locked up."

"Thank you both."

After the bookings, Zuma turned to Pat. "That's a first. I have never encountered a criminal with genuine remorse. On top of it, without an offer to reduce possible sentencing they express a desire to cooperate."

"Yeah, boss, I felt sorry for them."

"Pat, let's put our heads together and think of how they might help us. I don't want them locked up in our jails. If we can figure out a way to get their help, I'm sure the courts will look favorably upon them."

CHAPTER 28

Brotherly Love

"Boss, I'm waiting outside the condo. She carried the painting into the building. I saw the elevator go up to the floor he lives on. I'll wait for you. If either of them leaves, I'll detain them and tell them they have to go back in the house or upstairs or else come down to the station."

"Mr. and Mrs. Roy, Detective Zuma is on his way over, would you mind going back in and wait a few moments? We have a few questions that we want to ask you."

"You have no right to enter here unless you have a warrant. If you are not going to leave and let us do our errands, I'm going to call my lawyer right now."

"Call away."

"Boss, their lawyer is on the way. What should I do?"

"Just delay them. The lawyer can't make it ahead of me. Just wait with them outside."

"Mr. Vasquez, right now you are preventing me from freedom of movement. What are your grounds?"

"Look, if you don't like what I'm doing, let's go down to the station and I'll ask you some questions about a robbery. You are a suspect."

Roy laughed. "Wait till my lawyer hears this one. You are completely off base. You have no case against me because I never stole anything."

"That's fine. If it's true, you have no reason to worry."

"Do I have to stay also? I think if I were a suspect, your Zuma fellow would have asked me questions at the school fundraiser."

"Yes, Mrs. Roy, you also need to stay."

"And what grounds do you have against her?"

At that moment the lawyer and Zuma arrived.

"Hi, Detective, I'd like to speak to my clients in private for a few moments."

"Guy, we can do this here, outside, upstairs, or downtown at the precinct. He has a right to drag you in for questioning. I'll go with you, but I can't stop him. It would be easier, and I think would make you look better if we just do it here."

"I don't want to go back into the house. Let's do it right here."

"Detective, Mr. and Mrs. Roy, in the spirit of full cooperation, are willing to be questioned here and in my presence."

The lawyer and the Roys walked away and sat down on a bench.

"My client is willing to speak and explain how he came into possession of the painting. He assures me that he did not steal it. How can we make this official, just in case we do have to go to court?"

"Pat, will you record this and date it with names and place."

"Sure, boss."

"As my wife can testify, I am a bit of a health nut. I run on the bluffs and bike whenever I can. I was walking after a six-mile run and I saw this picture being painted of a hobo. It was special for me."

"Why is that?"

"It's my twin brother. My brother has been homeless for about ten years. He had a schizophrenic break and doesn't want to receive treatment. He prefers living in the street. He has been picked up many times for drug usage, creating a public disturbance, and other petty offenses. I often give him money when I am running on the bluffs and see him begging. I guess he uses it for drugs. I'm ashamed to say this. It's an embarrassment to me. I can't afford to have my clients know, and I do not want my children to know that their uncle is a beggar, a druggie, and homeless."

"So, when you saw the painting you were afraid?"

"Yes, that someone would see the strong resemblance between the two of us and start asking questions. I couldn't go up to the artist and ask her if she wanted to sell it because I knew she would spot the resemblance right away."

"What did you do then?"

"I asked my brother and promised him money if he would destroy the work. He tried apparently but failed. I didn't know he failed. I had given him money when he told me he had destroyed it by jumping and tearing it. I don't know if my brother lied or not. All I know is that when I saw it in the Shangri-La, I felt lucky. I felt I had an opportunity to own it and keep it hidden from the world. I believed my brother had lied to me about destroying the painting."

"So, you had nothing to do with how another hobo painting got to the fundraiser? And are you saying that your efforts to purchase the original painting at Shangri-La failed?"

"My efforts did fail, and I have no idea how the painting showed up at the fundraiser. I swear, Detective. I'm willing to take a lie detector on both of those."

"And why did you, Mrs. Roy, purchase the second hobo painting?"

I am aware of Guy's feelings about his brother. I couldn't tell you the truth. We do not want anyone to know about our embarrassment. I just happened to be there and saw the painting and knew what I should do to keep our family secret. I was pleased that I could do that for Guy and myself."

"Honey, you did well, but we failed. We only have two paintings. I bought one and it has the number four on it, and you picked up a second. Two of them are still out there."

"Mr. Roy, I can confirm that only one is out there. We had numbered your painting incorrectly on purpose to scare the purchaser. For what it's worth, the portrait of your brother is hanging somewhere in America."

"Maybe the artist will be willing to tell me to whom she sold it. I would be willing to pay for the information, and of course, I know it would be more."

"Your brother seems to be an ongoing expense for you, Mr. Roy. Perhaps you can think of another way of dealing with him?"

"Maybe, but right now I can afford it, and right now I would feel most comfortable if I could have all three paintings."

"Sweetheart, let's go back to the school and find out where the artist lives and get a phone number."

"I can give you that information, Mr. Roy. Before I do that, would you be willing to tell us why you own two residences?"

"Detective, that question does not seem related to the particulars of this case. I would urge my client to not answer."

"It's okay. First and foremost is that we can afford it. Property in this city is an excellent investment. I also like to have my clients visit in a more casual but elegant setting rather than the usual office. It's a condo that I use for some business deals. Angie uses her condo for her work, and she can also bring clients who want to purchase her photographs."

"And what kind of business deals are you engaged in Mr. Roy?"

"I'm a financial consultant specializing in helping provide information on philanthropies."

"Okay, Mr. Roy, here is the number you asked for. One more question. Your store, which sells banners trophies and uniforms, do you work in it?"

"No, I have a good manager who is full time. All our other employees are part time. I give students we have contacts, an opportunity to get sales experience. And since they work on a bonus system, I have no problem finding help."

"Thank you all for helping. I'd like the name of the manager of your store. I'll get the number for the artist who did the painting for you, Mrs. Roy. Goodbye for now."

"Boss, they sure cover their bases."

"They do, Pat. But I think they're covered with fancy horseshit that we are supposed to step in and get stuck. I'd like you to check out this trophy place and spend some time with the kids who work there and how they got their jobs, what their actual pay is, and see if this bonus system is in place. Maybe the bonus system is tied to something else besides selling uniforms."

"What makes you suspicious boss?"

"Why would rich kids from a private school need to work or want to work? Just for the experience? I'm sure their parents could find better jobs with richer experiences than just selling."

"You're right, boss. Those uniforms they sell could be the cover for something that smells rotten."

CHAPTER 29

A Hobo in America

Claudia told Joe immediately about the phone call. "What should I do?"

"Before I answer, let me give you the background to his phone call to you. I gave him your number because he would have gotten it from the school. This is official business, so you have to keep it between us."

"Of course. I like that you trust me with the details of your work."

Zuma described the brother's shame about his hobo twin brother including the wife's serendipitous purchase. "I'm not comfortable if you give out the number of your buyer. I am suspicious of this Roy character. And I until I know all about him, I think it's better not to get another innocent involved."

"Joe, all it might mean is that the Cape Cod owner could make more money and that Roy would feel better if the world does not know about his hobo brother. I like the idea of the painting being at the Cape, but he said he would give me five hundred for the information."

"That's an awful lot of money. Maybe not for him, but shame and embarrassment can be expensive. I guess it might be worth it to not have the world know his brother was a panhandler. I still prefer you keeping the information to yourself."

"Joe, what should I tell him?"

"Can you tell a white lie? Tell him the client has no interest in selling but if he changes his mind, he will call you?"

"Sure, Joe. I can do that. Maybe we can visit his hobo brother when we get back from the Cape this summer."

"Claudia, I know you named the painting 'Incompleteness' but I think of it now as 'A Brother's Shame.'"

I cannot change the name on the painting from 'Incompleteness' except in my head because it or he has traveled. I now think of it as 'A Hobo in America.' And, honey, you're in very good company because I think of your painting now along with the Woody Guthrie song about a hobo.

"I didn't know he had one."

Zuma sang the lyrics. *"I ain't got a home in this world anymore. No, I ain't got a home in this world anymore."* He relished his ability to remember the Guthrie ballad.

CHAPTER 30

More Drugs and More Schools

"Mr. Tapper, as we discussed earlier, I'm going to have to report you for having knowledge of drug use by your students and not reporting it."

"Thank you, Detective Zuma, for waiting until the fundraiser was over. We did well, and I'm ready to face the court. But I have some information that may help you in your search for drug dealers and sellers. I was hoping with this cooperation that I might be able to reduce the sentencing that is going to take place."

"Thank you, but we already know how opiates got into the school."

"I wasn't talking about opiates. I am talking about cocaine."

"I can't promise you anything, but I would be willing to put in a good word for you with the D A if your information proves to be valuable."

"It's about the parent who called me. Do you recall? His name was Guy Roy."

"Yes, I remember how you lowered the admission fees for his children."

"I'm sure it must have seemed strange to you that he was willing to settle for so little when you and I know he could have won a lot more money in suing the school."

"Maybe he did that because he has child in the school and that would make him look bad and his kid would bear the brunt of a lot of teasing and name calling. And, from what I see about his lifestyle, he doesn't really need money."

"And did you know that his lifestyle included an affair with our teacher, Hope Schnable?"

"Okay, and what does this have to do with drugs in your school?"

"Let me tell you. It's a bit of a long story. I saw Hope and Guy one afternoon in his car and they seemed pretty cozy, and when I confronted her about the dangers of an affair with a parent, she opened up. She told me that she had fallen in love with him and he had promised he would be leaving his wife. Shortly after the affair had begun, Guy suggested they try coke. She was open to this fancy, rich, and smooth guy. The fact that her lover knew about the world of art was a big plus for her. She said she saw it as a way to find a supporter of her desire to do her own art. When she told Guy about her selling opiates from her parents, he saw another opportunity and suggested that she could greatly increase her income if she would sell cocaine. She mentioned by that time, she was strongly addicted, dependent on him for coke, and also in love."

"So where does coke selling come in?"

"Hope got some of her kids to go to the other schools where they had friends and to deal. She picked four kids, and they each went to the other schools. They were all in Santa Monica."

"Did she tell you who the kids were?"

"No, she wouldn't do that?"

"I had to be careful in my efforts to find out who they were, but I wasn't successful. Hope began having second thoughts and she said she needed to stop. When Roy rejected her idea, she said she was going to his wife about the affair."

"And you never told this to anyone but me?"

"That's right. When she was murdered, I thought it was probably him. But I was afraid to let you know. He called and threatened me. I had to keep my mouth shut about my suspicions. If the police showed up at his door, he would report that I knew about student drug use. He said he would also tell the board about my tuition reduction and that I would probably be responsible for reimbursing the school. I didn't believe that threat, but I now knew that in addition to be a drug pusher he was a mean SOB."

"Mr. Tapper, you have been helpful. I'm not going to do anything as of this moment. Just sit tight for a few more days. And as before, don't leave the country."

"I'm still running a school, Detective, which I will do until I have to appear in court."

CHAPTER 31

A Welcome Divorce

"Pat, it's time to call the Schnables in. We may have a new chapter in our story I'm calling it 'Old People Strike Back.'"

"What did you have in mind, boss?"

"Let's get two wires and teach them how to be comfortable with it. Once they know how to work it, Mr. and Mrs. Roy will be getting a visit."

It took a while before they could get past the security guard in the condo, but when they mentioned that they were the parents of Hope, he let them in. Mrs. Roy was not there but Roy was not alone. A six-foot-four body-builder-type guy stood in the corner. Mrs. Schnable grabbed her husband's hand when she saw him. He stood looking at them, unreadable. Roy made no effort at an introduction. Mr. Schnable knew he had to lead off.

"Mr. Roy, we know that you know that our daughter was selling opiates, and we are now in trouble because it has been discovered that we were her supplier. Hope wrote to us and told us that she was in love with you and that she was hoping to be married."

"I never said anything to her about leaving my wife. I never promised that I would do that."

"Well, even if you didn't, you were and are married and we need money for our defense. Here is what we need. We need a top-flight expensive lawyer to minimize a jury's judgment about our breaking the law. We think that a case can be made to ensure that our sending opiates to Hope might be seen as helping our daughter."

"And why would I give you money?"

"Perhaps because we could tell your wife about Hope."

Roy needed to know if the Schnables knew anything else beyond the affair. If that's all they knew, he could risk his wife's wrath and even a divorce.

"I'm not going to respond to that threat. As a matter of fact, I might even welcome the divorce. And you can bet that when you come up for trial, I will use all my influence to insure you get as many years as you deserve."

"Let's go, honey. Mrs. Roy will be quite interested, and we have a chance to make Mr. Roy happy. Maybe Hope would have liked that we did that."

The bodyguard opened the door for their exit but still said nothing.

"That human being compared to Mr. Roy looked straight out of the death camps. I thought we had a monopoly on those types in Germany. Where did he find that iceman? We must tell Zuma."

"Honey, I just had a visit from the parents of the teacher who was killed. They believe that I had an affair with their daughter. No, of course I didn't. I think they are desperate for cash and they are trying to blackmail me. I think you should be expecting them. I would never have an affair. I love you so much."

"Mr. and Mrs. Schnable, you were perfect. Give us the wires. Pat, make a copy and put it away for safekeeping. You and I are going to pay a visit to Angie Roy and have her listen to the tape. Pat, can we put a tail on Mr. Roy? I want to find out who the damn iceman is. Get a picture or prints if you can so we can run them? He probably is a driver as well."

CHAPTER 32

A Vengeful Divorce

"Detective Zuma? Again? Okay. Let me change from my robe into something more decent. I'll be right there."

Angie Roy came back dressed to the nines. She was wearing black blouse and dark blue slacks. Zuma knew that the importance of clothing was something she shared with her husband. He could see she still had a great figure. She knew it and was not shy about using it as she walked in.

"Thanks for seeing us, Mrs. Roy. We have a tape we'd like you to listen to. I'd suggest that you sit down."

She sat quietly, listening with her face immobile. When it was done, she did not speak. Zuma could see her wheels turning. He imagined she was probably thinking about all the times he had called to say he would be delayed and unable to keep their appointment. Or the other times when he had stayed overnight at some place distant enough to not get home at all. When she spoke, it was steely and cold.

"What do you want me to do, Detective Zuma? If he is happy to get a divorce, I shall give to him. It will be one hell of a divorce."

"No, it's not about the divorce it's something else. First, please don't tell him what you now know. You can always say you never got a call from Hope's parents, and he may think they thought twice about doing anything. For now, just keep your cool if possible. Second, I will have the painter who did the hobo painting give you a call with the phone number of the buyer and we can go from there."

"What good will those do me?"

"It may lead to more serious charges against him than an affair, which would help you in any divorce battle."

"Okay, Detective, I'm in. Count on me. What might also help Detective Zuma is if you were to look into the years before his first marriage, the marriage itself, and the divorce."

"How might that help in this case?"

"I think it could. That is all I want to say for now."

"Thank you, Mrs. Roy. I'll give you a call with the phone number. If you have any questions, here's my card."

On the ride back to the office, Pat expressed his confusion. "Boss, You're ahead of me."

"I know. I think I'm even ahead of myself. Put a twenty-four-hour watch on the condo. Get the name from security of everyone who signs in. We have a murderer to catch, a robbery to solve, and lots of guilty people: two foreign-born childless parents, a school principal, a possible high-end drug dealer, a bodyguard, four children, and ex-boyfriends. We also have two vics, so far, and I'm worried that there will be more. We need to get every piece of information we can get from newspaper and magazine articles and official documents about Guy Roy."

The toothpick was out, and the humming started.

CHAPTER 33

Wind Beneath Me

"Boss, Claudia called. She said it was not urgent, but she would like you to call back when you get her message."

"Honey, please come home. The rain stopped. The sun is out. It is clear and gorgeous. I would love to take a walk with you on the beach. We have one hour before sunset."

Joe told Pat he was leaving early. He no longer felt he had to or should put work first. He had done that with Carol, but now with Claudia, he had told himself he would never do it again.

The sand was wet but still firm enough to walk on without a struggle. The white clouds were turning pink and pinker with raised white waves crashing steadily as the sun neared the horizon.

"Joe, isn't this heavenly? Gorgeous and wild, totally untamed and untamable."

"A bit like you, darling."

Claudia smiled and pushed her arm closer into his side. "You have tamed me, dear sir."

They waited till the sun just dipped behind the horizon and then went to dinner at the Shangri-La.

"Claudia, I want to tell you something that I had never told anyone about. It had started after Carol was killed. I began listening to Randy Newman sing "I think It's Gonna Rain Today." At first, I couldn't quite figure out why it meant so much to hear those words. After listening to Newman sing, I began listening to the other versions and interpretations of Newman's song. Barbara Streisand, Joe Cocker, and Bette Midler had all recorded this song with its sad, dark words. The version that struck the deepest chord of sadness in me was the one by Nina Simone. I marveled at the genius of Newman but also how these other talented folks could take that genius and do something that would not detract from the original and would add to it and be different. Slowly, I began to figure out why they meant so much to me.

"A pale dark moon in a sky streaked with grey was what I myself had often loved seeing in the heavens. In the phrase, 'Human kindness is overflowing,' I felt the irony that Newman recognized. He saw that our world where human kindness is lacking was driven by greed and the hunger for power. The song kept repeating that it was always going to rain. The rain would never stop, and I would never have to be surprised about the number of murderers. The rain would not stop. 'I think its gonna rain today.'

"The fake and phony smiles of the murderers I captured were like the 'frozen smiles of the scarecrows that chased love away.' I frequently listened to Nina Simone's rendition. Her singing the last word 'Lonely' made me think of Carol. Carol was the embodiment of the words, 'Bright before me, the signs implore me, help the needy and show them the way.' Carol had been the one who convinced me that I was helping and protecting the needy and the innocent. Even though I knew that it would be raining tomorrow and the next day.

"Joe, that is so lovely. I'm glad for you that you had that with Carol."

"Me too, but I don't listen to that as frequently as I did. I have two new ones that I listen to now that you are in my life."

"Which ones, Joe?"

"Well, since you are the seeds of my love, for you I play 'The Rose' and since you are my strength, I play "You Are the Wind Beneath My Wings."

"Joe, the songs that I always hummed before we met had to do with dreams. 'I'm Dreaming of a White Christmas,' 'Dream a Little Dream,' 'Impossible Dream,' and 'All I Have to do is Dream.' I don't hum them anymore. My impossible dream has come true." Claudia paused and looked at Joe with love and adoration in her eyes. "So, pay the bill and let's go home so I can be beneath your wings. Ain't nothing impossible about that."

CHAPTER 34

A Call from Truro

"Joe, I just got a call. A Detective Malloy from Truro wanted to know what my calls to the chap who bought my painting were about."

"How would he know you called him? What did you tell him?"

"I told him that I would prefer that he speak to you as you were also a detective."

"This is Detective Zuma calling from the Santa Monica Police Department. I'm responding to your call to my wife."

Zuma listened attentively, jotting down notes.

"Here is what I know. Your corpse visited a restaurant in Santa Monica and bought my wife's painting. A few days ago, someone contacted her and wanted to purchase it. She told him she would have to call the buyer, that's your person in Truro. My wife told the interested party that the painting was, at this point, not for sale but might be available at some point in the future."

"Can you give me a description of the painting? Nothing seemed stolen or broken. Whoever killed the guy seemed to have entered, used his weapon, and left. It didn't seem like a burglary, just a murder. No prints on anything. No suspects. No one saw anything or heard the shot. Must have had a muzzle. Seems like a professional. The guy who was murdered was an art collector, ran a gallery in Provincetown and was liked by his neighbors."

"It was a painting of a hobo. The background is the ocean, our ocean, the Pacific."

"I'll send my guys out to check for it. As soon as I know anything, I'll get back to you."

"Boss, how did they get Claudia's phone number?"

"They found a cell phone next to the body and began calling all the recent numbers."

"Boss, that's three bodies and three paintings. Is it possible that there is a connection?"

"I know, there has to be a connection and someone, somehow must have figured out how to get to the third painting. It had to be Roy. It's a professional hit. Don't know if he did it or hired someone."

"Detective Zuma? There was nothing in the art collection that came close to looking like a hobo. I had my guys check the gallery also. We found nothing. What can you tell me about this painting? There were a lot of very expensive works in the house that were not touched."

"All I can say at this point is the person who wants to own all the paintings of the hobo that my wife did says he is embarrassed because the hobo is his brother. As he is in the public limelight, he feels it would be damaging to his reputation and image and hurt his business."

"Embarrassed enough to kill?"

"If I were right in my hunches, it would not be the first. It's a long way from Santa Monica to Truro but saving your business and reputation makes the distance negligible."

"Let me know if I can do anything more on this end."

"I will. I'm glad you followed up the phone calls and we made contact. Our paths may cross again. I'm pretty sure I will be vacationing again this summer at the Cape."

"I'll get back to you after we check out the gallery and maybe that could help you a bit more. And I look forward to meeting you this summer. Goodbye for now, Detective Zuma. I have got to figure out how to answer the questions from our TV station wondering why there are no leads and speculating it's the summer workers who are mostly Middle Easterners, Russians, and Italians."

"Looks like you have to deal with the same xenophobic crap in Cape Cod that we do in sunny California."

CHAPTER 35

Loving Latinas

"Boss, we hit the jackpot. Mrs. Roy was right. There's a goldmine on Roy."

"Let's hear it, Pat."

"First marriage. He marries a Latina. She's seventeen and from a very rich Spanish family. Old time Californians. Their clan, Garcia, was respected and powerful in real estate, banking, and farming. There's an engagement picture and an announcement. Nothing on his family. In a wedding picture, it looks like Roy's brother was best man. The bride is hardly a looker and quite heavy. I imagine she fell completely in love or luck to have this suitor. At seventeen, with her looks and weight, I doubt she could have had much experience. They had twins about seven months after the marriage. Divorce papers are filled right after that. The divorce is all over the papers with Guy wanting half of the property that was given to his bride (probably worth half a million) plus $150,000 that was a gift to the wife. The old man was holding the money until a child was born. According to the coroner's report, the wife dies from an overdose. The case goes to court and the prosecution accuses Guy of false intentions and evidence of lovers both prior and post marriage. The court proceedings are stopped after the prosecution's opening statement. Next thing we know is that Guy is appearing in California living a high lifestyle, lots of dames, a yacht, and real estate purchases."

"What's your guess as to why the case stopped?"

"The money was not the issue. I think the old man wanted to ruin his reputation and embarrass him as much as possible. He had lost his daughter and was probably thinking about the twins."

"What happened to the twins?"

"The old man adopted them. Changed their surname back to the family name. Their names are Edwin and Edward. We don't know where they are now. Their names don't appear anywhere after the court proceedings. There is an obituary on the old man with the survivors being 'two grandchildren.'"

"Have you tried to locate them?"

"Boss, Garcia is an extremely common name. Even with their first names and narrowing down the search, we are going to have to assign someone else to make more than six hundred calls."

"Pat, pick one of our rookies. That's the kind of good police work that we do. Do we know anything more about how Roy made his money?"

"You're on the trail, boss. He was a co-investor in buying a huge construction business. Three days after the deal was signed, the partner drops dead of a heart attack. He is now sole owner. The family sues but he walks away as sole owner. It seems that there was a clause that each of them would become sole owner if the other passed away or was incapable of fulfilling responsibilities."

"Pat, this is very weird. After wife number one dies from an overdose, he walks away with a bundle of cash, and after the partner dies, his bundle is increased. This new business is rich on paper. There is no immediate cash. He doesn't sell it. He buys into it with cash from wife. He has little or nothing left. In my mind, there's a lot of money unaccounted for. How does he acquire all these other real estate holdings?"

"I don't know, boss. Marriage number two is very quiet. No pictures in the papers. Court documents revealed a witness signature, male, same last name as Roy. Angie Fernandez, (this guy really goes for the Latinas) is very wealthy. There is a prenup signed where any money or property held by the couple prior to their union shall remain as such. All income generated from business or investments from the date of the marriage shall be community property."

"So, the condos belong to both of them."

"That's correct, boss."

"I guess that Angie doesn't have a lot to lose in a divorce and neither does he."

"Seems that way. But they do have a very expensive lifestyles, one that would be difficult to maintain on investments alone."

"I think we need tax returns. I have to figure out a way to get Roy to come down to the station even if he brings his mouthpiece. I need him to sweat."

CHAPTER 36

Lost Children

"How did you find me, Detective?"

"Lots of effort. We called pretty much every E. Garcia using the internet living in the Los Angeles area. We were lucky you answered the phone. So, you're Edward. Glad to meet you."

"What can I do for you? You mentioned my father. I have nothing to do with him. He abandoned us, and I don't even think of him as a dad. Our grandfather raised us and told us about this douchebag of a dad. My sister and I agreed a long time ago he was not worth pursuing. We've seen his pictures and figured he's doing with this second wife what he did to our mother."

"Which is?"

"Screwing her out of money. Knowing him, as I think I do, wife number two is also going to die from an overdose."

"Edward, we are investigating him for a number of illegal matters, which I cannot reveal to you now. But I want to know if you would be willing to help us?"

"Absolutely. You can't count on my sister. She is limited in her abilities. She was born with some special needs, and I think she was an embarrassment to him."

"Well, that might work to our advantage. Edward, would you be willing to see a therapist that I can recommend? I have used him before in investigations. He will respect any confidence you share with him. He is a responsible and decent fellow. He will not try and make you see your dad but would help you explore any feelings that you may still harbor. I have a hunch that seeing him might help our investigation. The therapist won't tell Roy of your visit, but I suspect he will somehow find out. That might make him jumpy which could help us. Of equal importance is that it might help you. Right now, I see anger."

"You see correct. If you think this might help get him into trouble, I will agree. But I can't guarantee that my sister or I would want to see him."

"I don't need a guarantee. Thank you for doing this. The name of the doc is Jerry Milgram. As I said, I have used him before, and he is a man of integrity. Here's his number. I'll call him and tell him to expect your call.

"Dr. Milgram? This is Detective Zuma. Yes, it has been a while. I am going to ask your help with something that is a bit out of the ordinary. Would you be willing to see a young man of thirty or so who was abandoned by his father when he was less than a year? There is a twin, a special-needs sister. He said he would be willing to talk with you about his dad. He has not seen him and only knows about him from the papers. His mother? She died about three years after their birth. At least that's the way it was reported. A second child was born but dies shortly after. The ME said the infants' body was filled with drugs."

"And what exactly are you expecting from me, Detective?"

"Ideally, I would hope his talk with you might convince him to confront his father, but I know that you can't require or force him to do that. A second-best thing would be to have him available later on, if I need him in a trial. His discussion of the consequences of his abandonment might convince a jury about Roy's character. I don't need to know anything until such time as a trial might require the DA's office to subpoena your notes."

"I'd be happy to see the young man."

"Thank you, Dr. Milgram. You should be expecting a call from Edward Garcia."

Milgram was pleased to get this call from Zuma. Working on cases that were outside his practice excited him and though this was going to be straightforward therapy sessions, he hoped it might branch out into the kind of work he had done earlier with Zuma. In that case, a son and patient of his was going to confront his brother about the possible murder of their mom and Milgram was afraid that his patient would commit murder. He had accompanied his client and actually prevented a possible murder. He and Zuma had coordinated their efforts, which resulted in the capture of the murderer.

"Hi, Mr. Garcia. Yes, Detective Zuma told me to expect your call. I can see you any evening after six. I would also like you to bring your sister along. Well, if she is not willing, then, of course not. If she changes her mind and decides she would like to join you, I would welcome her."

CHAPTER 37

Underage and Undercover

"Pat, place one of our baby-face rookies in the school. I've gotten Tapper to allow it and the DA's office has agreed. We need to find out who the kids are who were working for Hope and who has replaced her as their supplier. As smart as these kids are, they still are kids and like to show off their money. Have him figure out who the runners of coke are. He should be able to do that. Do you think we have someone who could pass as eighteen years old? No weapons. Just good snooping."

"I'm on it, boss. I know just the rookie."

"You'll need to call Tapper and alert him so the rookie can show up with the proper transfer papers. No one else is to know about this except him. After you do that, let's pay a visit to Mr. Romantic. I think there are too many loose ends floating around in my head."

"All right, Jack, let's go over this again. Your work verified that you left at five and the lady in the hallway said she saw you around six as she was going to dinner. You said that you had stopped in to pick up some food and ate it and watched Maddow on the tube. Maddow is on between six and seven. Did you catch most of her show?"

"I don't think so. I know I saw her and the famous ending she gives to her show before introducing Laurence O'Donnell."

"Did you go out after eating at home?"

"No, Detective, I was wiped from work and must have nodded off by about eight or so."

"Had you seen Lisa since she returned?"

Zuma realized he had not asked him about that possibility.

"I offered to pick her up when she arrived. At first, she said no. But I was adamant. When I met her, I asked her if she wanted to grab a bite before I dropped her off. And she agreed. I took her to this neat little place on Manchester Boulevard called Truxton's. We arrived and we managed to get a quiet booth in the back of the restaurant. I asked her if she could forgive me and she got quiet. She stared at me with a puzzled and bewildered look. She cocked her head to one side as if to make sure who I was or what I was saying. Before she could say anything, I took out the ring that I had been planning to give her. She looked at it and started to laugh. I asked her what was so funny, and she stood up on top of the table and began screaming out loud so everyone, not only those near our table but everyone, could hear her.

"'Hey, ladies and gentlemen. This jerk is asking me to marry him after I found out he's been screwing around on me. Is there anyone here in this restaurant that thinks I should? Wouldn't you all think I'm stupid for believing him now? He lied earlier.'

"People stopped eating and looked up. They were hushed now. Most of the women were smiling. It was a show. Some guy yelled out, 'Lady why don't you give him another chance.'

"'Oh, look who gives advice about another chance. Let me ask that lady you're eating with if she would give you a second chance.'

"Lisa is fuming now. She has the attention of everyone, even the wait staff and folks working the counter. She is beginning to relish what she is doing. She screams again. 'Is there any woman in this restaurant, is there one single woman who would give her man a second chance? There is utter silence. Lisa takes the ring in her hand and holds it up and is still screaming. Everyone is rapt.

"'Everyone, look at this ring that I'm holding in my hand. I am going to give this ring to the woman who will forgive her two-timing boyfriend.' Not a single woman raised her hand. 'Since none of you would let them back in, I'm going to sell this thing. Here is

94

my e-mail. I need to hear from you in the next ten minutes. When I get your names, I will divide the money into equal shares for all of us. Make sure you give me your address and I will send you a check. Now, let me introduce you to this person. You should all know him. His name is Jack, Jack Wembley. You can now know him as Jack the Jerk Wembley. Isn't he a wondrous thing? He gives rings to women he has lied to and cheated on. Do they keep the rings, Jack? Is this the same one you gave to the last woman you proposed to? Jack, you are really something. Because now you are going to give money to women whom you have never screwed. To women you have never lied to. I'm sure, Jack, that all the women in this restaurant will appreciate you. Look ladies, he will be giving you all money.' She began screaming. 'Fuck you and your childish, immature, sophomoric, hurtful, misogynous, distressing, juvenile, and babylike behavior.'

"Lisa got down from the top of the table, stepped out of the booth, and just walked out slowly. All the women in the restaurant stood up and applauded as she strode out. I sat there and could not look up. Even some of the men were laughing. After a while, I threw some money on the table. As I walked out with my head down, a woman said, 'Thanks for the money, Jack.' A few of the men said things like 'She's a tough broad, Jack' and 'You got a real ball buster, Jack.'"

"What did you do after she left?"

"I sat in the car and thought of how I could get her back. I couldn't believe she was that angry with me and believed she must have had other feelings for me. I waited until I thought she would be home, and I started calling. After about ten efforts, she picked up. 'Jack, you prince. Nine women called. You made nine women happy. But not the one you wanted to marry. So, you are their Prince Charming. But Jack, you're my Prick Charming. Don't you ever bother calling me.'

"She also said that if I called her again, she would get a stalking complaint."

"Did you ever see her again?"

"No, Detective."

"How come you didn't tell us the first time we interviewed you?"

"You got to be kidding me, Detective. This was the most humiliating thing that ever happened to me. I also didn't want to say something idiotic and typical like, 'I learned my lesson about cheating.' But the truth is I did. I wish I hadn't made those stupid mistakes."

"Okay. You did say you owned a gun. Would you be willing to let us run some ballistics on it?

"Sure, Detective. I know I hurt Lisa deeply I regret it. But I didn't kill her."

CHAPTER 38

Planting Seeds

"Hi, Detective Zuma, this is Dr. Milgram. I have spent a few sessions with Edward Garcia. I can have a report ready for you if you need it."

"What can you tell me off the record for now?"

"He is a pretty damaged person, but he is able to hide it from the world and he functions well. He covers up a lot of his feelings of sadness and hurt. He feels cheated about opportunities, as he has been a caretaker to his sister. No, I didn't see her. She did not want to speak to any shrink."

"Do you think he might want to confront his dad?"

"He was much more willing to think about that possibility when we finished our work than when we began. I don't know. If I had to put money on it, I would say it's a good possibility. I left it with him that if he decided that he wanted to do that, he should come in so we could discuss what he might say and what he wanted to get out of the confrontation. Do I think he is dangerous? I think that there is that possibility, especially if his dad acts like the big jerk he has always been and starts to belittle Edward."

"Dr. Milgram, I have seen that man in different situations, and he belittles everyone. I'm sure Edward has his buttons."

"Mr. Roy knows what they are since he planted them in Edward."

Zuma dwelled on the last phrase of parents implanting sensitive spots inside their children that would always know would be there.

He thought it was not only parents who could do this but also friends and lovers. The seeds for sadness, hurt, and even bitterness could be inserted at any time by anyone. He had learned what they were with Carol and now Claudia. He knew what they were with Pat. He felt that his work as a detective allowed him to remove those who had already created hopelessness for many and capturing them would stop them.

CHAPTER 39

No More Selling

"Boss, this is Private Jensen. He's been working the school beat."

"Welcome, Jensen. Glad to meet you face to face. How did your work go?"

"It went well, sir. I got the names of the students who went to each of the schools. They do like to flash their money around and often treat others at the school with goodies at Starbucks or Coffee Bean."

"Were you part of those who drank freely?"

"Yes, I was, sir."

"Well, I guess we won't hold it against you that you were eating cookies and drinking lattes on the job while you were getting paid."

They all laughed.

"Thank you, sir. I also picked up that their selling had dropped off lately. There were a few jokes about the visits to Starbucks becoming much less frequent since the teacher was killed. The ones who I thought were selling the drugs didn't think this comment was so funny and got huffy when they heard it. They made a few comments like how anyone can think this great teacher could do anything like that. You know, sir, like they were guilty and had been caught."

"Good work, Jensen. We'll take the names and go from here. Pat, you and I are going to see Tapper and make sure that he gets the word out on Jensen that his parents moved suddenly because of a job offer and that is why he is no longer in school. We need to see Tapper about these kids."

"Mr. Tapper, we have the names of the kids who were going to the other schools and selling. If we pull them in, their parents are going to raise a storm and all kinds of lawsuits are going to fly. Parents at the other schools will start to raise havoc and we are going to have the biggest shit storm in education since the famous preschool child molesting incident in the early 80s. It was called the McMartin Case and it cost taxpayers a fortune since it was in the courts for over two years. Nothing ever came of that, and I'm afraid that with the kind of weight, these parents have that nothing can come of this. Mr. Tapper, I don't want to see my department or your school in shambles, tons of parents and four schools in an uproar, lawsuits upon lawsuits over what four rich kids did."

"I think that is very thoughtful of you, Detective Zuma. I do want to point out however that while no one was ever found guilty in the case you cited, child molestation was put into the nation's awareness. You and I know that the problems you uncovered at my school probably occur at every school in America."

"I know that. I'm aware of that. And maybe my keeping it relatively quiet is a Band-Aid. But it is a choice I'll make at this time. It's a choice we make daily in our work. Do we deal with users and petty dealers or put our energy into the big dealers? You know my answer. We don't arrest every homeless person who jay walks or who urinates in public. If we did that, we would have no manpower left to deal with murderers and robbers." Zuma thought of Claudia's image of the Bosch painting and how he had to deal with the bad stuff that was underground in the city and how he had to break concrete. This stuff with the kids could be in a Hopper painting that captured the loneliness of urban life and replaced it with the isolation of kids' lives. The kids' loneliness had been replaced with the Internet and drugs.

"What do you propose, Detective Zuma?"

"Actually, Mr. Tapper, I was going to ask you what you would propose to do. Something that would not create the shit storm that you and I know might happen if we don't handle this correctly but that will also stop the selling."

"What if I called them into my office, had you there and told them we know what they have done. We tell them we want it to stop. We make sure you tell them that. We can even offer them help if they think they need it. We are going to give them this chance to not be suspended, save their families from embarrassment, save themselves from going to a juvenile facility. If they are not willing, we will try and get the DA to consider their being tried in adult court which would mean a prison term if they are found guilty."

"Mr. Tapper, I think that might work. We'll keep Jensen in the schools. He'll be able to tell if they continue. Set it up. I may bring a therapist I know."

CHAPTER 40

A Lead from Truro

"Boss, we got a call from Detective Malloy from Truro. They checked all the rental cars from Logan Airport that were returned after one or two days and matched the names with the motels in the Wellfleet-Truro area. You won't believe this but the name that matches is Roy, but it is not Guy Roy it is Edward Roy."

"Could it be Edwin, by mistake? That's an awful lot of Roys we have to deal with. A regular royal pain in the ass."

"Good one, boss. Well, the address on the car registration was the same one that Guy lives in here in Santa Monica."

Edward doesn't live there. Only Edwin and Guy."

"Well, it's either Guy with a fake ID or that bodyguard who may be related. He could be another child. We are going to have to pay a visit."

"Gosh, Detective, seems like you just can't stay away."

"Yes, and I would like to be introduced to your chauffer bodyguard and cross-country traveler."

"Edwin, say hello to Detective Zuma and his associate, Mr. Vasquez."

Edwin nods.

"Your man last Friday took a flight from LAX to Logan, rented a car, and stayed in a motel in Wellfleet on the day there was a murder and a painting was stolen."

"All quite interesting, Detective. Are you here to discuss a traveling itinerary? Are you accusing Edwin of murder or are you going to arrest him? If you are planning to arrest him, I will call my lawyer right now and we will meet you at the jail. If you're not going to arrest him, I would like you to leave. I will point out that you have no gun and no witness. I'm sure you will see how reasonable all of this is if you knew the facts."

"What are the facts, Mr. Roy?"

"I wanted the painting. I was convinced that the seller would be willing to make a generous profit on his purchase. I sent someone I knew along with cash to purchase the painting. When he got to the house of the owner, it had already been set out as a crime scene."

"Edwin, would you tell me what your relationship is to Guy?"

Edwin looks at Guy who nods his head as if to say, "You can answer."

"He's my father."

"Did you travel to Truro to collect the painting?"

"The interview is over, Detective Zuma. Edwin does not have to answer any questions about his travels unless you are charging him and want to bring him down to your station. Unless your questions pertain to the murder or murders, I see no need for me to respond further."

"I do have one more question not related to our investigation. What is so important about owning the same painting?"

"We art collectors are a strange lot. Who can understand the motives we have when it comes to children, art, and family?"

"Boss, this guy is weird. He gives me the creeps. Three kids with names beginning with E and all having the same first syllable. *Ed*na, *Ed*win, and *Ed*ward, both wives are Latinas, and wife number two is also an *Ed*na. It's really creepy that he would he have his son as a bodyguard."

"Not only that. Two of the kids want nothing to do with their dad and the other is glued to him. What could a parent do to create these opposite reactions? I think I need to call Milgram about this."

CHAPTER 41

An All-Roy Meeting

"Hi, Edward. I'm glad you called, and I think you should be given an award for bravery for doing this."

"I'll probably get a purple heart after visiting the son of a bitch."

"Edward, you're going to see your father, and you need to keep in mind the two questions that are important to you. Why you were abandoned and why he never reached out to you. Those are what to keep in mind on your visit. Do not call him names and do not blow your stack. That would be too easy on him. It will only convince him that he made the right decision. You need to be cool. Try and remember everything he says. When do you see him?"

"This afternoon. He made it clear he have about fifteen minutes. That's almost a minute per year. Not exactly trying to make up for lost time."

"You need to face the very real possibility, Edward, that he doesn't want you in his life. It might be exactly the same for him now as it was then. He doesn't want to be involved or be close or be connected to you. If you go in with that expectation, you will not be disappointed."

"I don't know what to call you. I know what not to call you and that is 'Dad.'"

Guy stared at his progeny. He was good looking and seemed strong. He was sure that he worked out. In light of how Guy thought most twenty-two-year-olds would act in a similar situation, Edward seemed remarkably confident.

"Call me, Guy. Now tell me why you wanted to see me."

Edward who had been standing all this time, took a seat. The three of them were like the points of a triangle.

"Edward, meet Edwin. Edwin, meet Edward."

Edwin, who had been standing, took a seat. The two brothers stared at one another. No emotions passed their face. Edwin has a quizzical look. He feels he is staring into a mirror.

"Okay, Guy, here are the two questions I would like answered. Why did you abandon my sister and me and why didn't you see us over the years?"

"Nothing mysterious or hidden about the answers to those two questions. I married into a very wealthy Latina family. I was the gringo outsider. They tried hard to make me feel that I was part of the family, but I knew that I would never be considered as one of them. I did not have Latino blood. They were a very tight clan, well established, and successful. Their roots go back even before California became a state. No matter how much I rose in their family businesses, I thought I would always be seen as the gringo dude who married the gal who probably no one else would have married. Your grandfather made this clear when the two of you were born by assigning a large portion of his wealth and holdings to the two of you to be presented at a certain age."

When Guy uttered the phrase the "two of you," the boys looked at each other with a quizzical stare.

"And he even stipulated that you were to receive this only if you were to marry Latinos. This made it clear to me that they had no desire to allow you to assimilate. I needed to make it without family ties or people believing that I hadn't earned it. After about three years, I was determined to leave. I was doing very little for the family business, and I asked him how much it was worth to him if I left without the kids. I left after I was paid off by grandpa to leave. He got rid of me by paying me. You might even say he bought the two of you, and I sold the two of you. It was easy to stay away given that I knew he would be raising you to stay in that culture. I did not feel I could win you over to the importance of assimilation. I guess I was too busy with building a business and career to be involved. I was selfish."

"And so, you threw us out."

"Woah. I abandoned you but did not throw you into the dustbin. You were also brown skinned, and I thought I would be hampered in my business."

"Selfish, greedy, and racist. What a dad. *Maybe* it was better that you abandoned us."

"That's what I thought and have been trying to tell you. I believed you would be better off without me being part of your lives."

"How much money did you get for the two of us? You selfish, money-hungry, greedy, bastard? You didn't even stick around for my mother's funeral."

"I'm sure grandpa filled your head with lots of tales about my selfish ways. I still am selfish, but you are not a bastard. And I assume that Grandpa left you assets to keep you comfortable."

"I'm not going to tell you anything about my life or your daughter's. You have no right to know anything about us. And I don't believe you're interested."

"As you wish."

Edward walked out staring at Edwin. Roy had already turned his back and was heading towards his desk. Edwin winked at Edward and put his hand to his ear, which indicated he would call.

CHAPTER 42

A New Class at SurePaths

The Schnables were sitting at breakfast with their meager meal of toast and coffee.

"We are stuck in this godforsaken country that took our daughter, and we have to wait until we hear from Zuma. Our stipends from Germany aren't allowing us to eat or live well."

"I have been feeling the same things. Since we're already in trouble and are counting on Zuma's testifying that we were helpful, I was wondering what we might do while we wait."

"Maybe we could volunteer at the school that Hope taught at. We could teach German, and if they even just let us eat in the cafeteria, that would help. And—"

"I think I know what you're going to say."

"Okay. You say it."

"Pick up where Hope left off."

"Yes, we could get a new prescription here for ourselves and continue to receive the old prescription from Germany. That would give us something to start with. The profits would be minimal, but we could at least have more food. And if those programs about drug use in American high schools are true, they would still be buying even after Hope was murdered. We could give Zuma the names of the kids who buy."

"I'm not sure that idea is a good one. We better check with Zuma."

"No, I think he'll stop it. He's too smart. Let's just do it. If he finds out, he finds out. If he asks us to stop, we stop."

"Well, that is very kind of you to offer to teach German. Yes, we could use this in our curriculum. And you are sure that you are willing to do this without compensation? Okay, you both are invited to eat your lunches every day in the cafeteria with the students. The teachers bring their own food."

"We can teach individually or coteach. If we coteach, we can do conversations, which would help the children learn faster."

"I like that. But you can't simply walk into a classroom in California. You have to be medically examined. A background check needs to be made. You probably will have to be interviewed. Your status as visitors who are applying for work may also become an issue. If you are willing to go through all of that, I will put you in a classroom. It would be no problem if I limited the two you to one afternoon a week. I can advertise it as a class for students who wanted to learn conversational German language. Give me a week to get a course description out. If you get through all the paperwork, that would help you take a group with you to visit and travel in Germany during the summer as a kind of study-abroad program. Depending on the size, we would also have to have other adults supervising. Yes, we would love to be able to do that as well."

"Joe, Hope's parents will be doing volunteer teaching at the school. It will be a conversational German language class. I guess they feel like they want to continue doing what their daughter did, teach and educate."

"Claudia, I am very doubtful if their motives are to just teach and educate. Remember, they are liars and drug dealers. I could stop it, but maybe they will turn up something further on the kids or dealers. I have an undercover in the school already, and I'm going to keep him there. He probably always wanted to learn German. Isn't Jensen a German name?"

"I will be amazed no matter how much cement you are able to break through, Joe, if you discover he has a German background."

CHAPTER 43

Stepbrothers United

"You're going to find this pretty hard to believe but I'm your stepbrother. Our dad never mentioned anything about other children. It was only by searching on Google that I found out he had two other children from his first marriage. And I have a stepsister also, correct?"

"Yes, she is a twin her name is Edna. She is a special-needs person."

"When I first saw you, I couldn't believe it."

"Neither could I. I had to control myself from not rushing over to you and giving you a hug. I'm the younger one and always wanted an older brother to look up to."

"Well, how was it for you to hear your brother calling him those names? The selfish bastard didn't seem to be upset. And neither did you. I couldn't smile as I wanted to. He would have really been pissed off. I am pretty much forbidden from expressing anger or even disagreeing with him."

"Maybe I was one of the few who did."

"Actually, you're the only one I have ever seen. I was really impressed. And when I thought my stepbrother was doing this, I was really proud. It was stronger from you than it would have been from a stranger. You're family."

"You never disagree or disobeyed?"

"I can't remember the last time. No, he is a strict disciplinarian. No, I would say he's a cruel disciplinarian. My mom, your stepmom,

I suppose, helped me and made him go less often to the strap or bamboo. I have several scars to show for it. It was a very tight ship. He likes to feel he is totally in charge and he's the captain. Orders must be followed."

"But what was all that Latino hatred about? Even though he seems to have something against brown people, he married another Latina?"

"I think her money overshadowed her background. Her green made him overlook her brown. It's lucky I am light. If I were as dark as you, he would have probably handed me over to foster care. She might have fought him on that, but he already had her money so he wouldn't care. He would have set it up, as "I don't want him on my ship. If you do, you both can leave.""

"Wow, he really is as bad as I said."

"Yup, he sure is."

"I am around now to do whatever he asks. I have my own room, no rent, steady income but I'm pretty much on call."

"It's like you're the doctor and he's the patient."

"It's more like he's the master and I'm the slave."

I just had to go to Cape Cod and fly back. I had strict orders of where to stay, where I had to rent a car from, where I could drive, and how far to drive it."

"That sounds pretty weird."

"On his best days, he is weird. And there aren't too many best days for our father."

"There has got to be a way for you to get free. Even if he disowned you, you would have your freedom."

"He would make it impossible for me to get a job. He would probably figure out a way to frame me for something."

"He would do that to his own flesh and blood?"

"Sure, why not? Since when has flesh and blood mattered to him? Look at you." He paused. "I rest my case."

"Well, how can we get the SOB? Is there a way we can set a trap for him? There must be something we can do."

"He loves money. He loves power. He loves his reputation."

"Well, since we don't have money and power, our only plan would be to damage his reputation."

"Men's reputations can be destroyed when there are charges of sexual abuse, harassment, or child molestation."

"I don't know any women. I am close to my mother and less so to a few of her friends. I don't think any of her friends could be convinced to bring charges. And I don't think my mother would go for this idea."

"The only other woman I know is my sister."

"She was just three and a half when he left. You're not suggesting…oh my god."

"He won't be the first pervert to have played with a three-year-old."

"Would your sister be willing to do this?"

"Right now, I think she would rather murder him."

CHAPTER 44

Reputations and Power

"No, I never got a call from that couple. But I do have something you want. I'll come upstairs to talk with you."

"Edna, would you like a drink? Coffee or something stronger?"

"I have another painting of the hobo."

"You did that quickly. How did you get it?"

"I have my ways, Guy, as you have yours. Now, how much would you be willing to pay?"

"I will be most generous and give you $10,000 dollars."

"You're going to have to be can more generous than that. I want $20,000."

He had never quite seen his wife so determined but he didn't care to argue further, and he wanted the painting.

"That's over a five hundred percent increase from the original sale price, but even with that insane increase I'll write you a check right now."

"No, I want cash."

"You'll have to wait. I need to go down to the bank and get it for you."

"I'll wait here."

Guy was puzzled. She must have something else on her mind to make the money this important or to make him feel that she was in charge.

"Edwin, will you stay here with your mom and see that she is comfortable? I'll just have to take the elevator down to my bank. I won't be gone very long."

"Mom, are you angry at Dad? Has he done something to you?"

"Nothing that's very different from the past. But I am trying to put my foot down on his shenanigans."

"Mom, I met my stepbrother. He showed up and we didn't talk, but I contacted him after he left, and we met."

"Good for you, one less secret in the Roy clan. How was it? What did you talk about?"

"We talked about my mistreatment and he was pretty angry at Guy and called him all kinds of names. I loved that part. We also talked about how we might get back at him for—"

Guy enters the room.

"Here is the cash. I got it in big bills. How did you enjoy your private time together?"

"Guy, cut the crap. You're not really interested in our time together unless it's going to affect you. Here is something that is going to affect you. I gather another one of your ways was an affair and lying to me. And what are you willing to pay for me to not go to court and have it brought out that this wonderful businessman and philanthropist was screwing a teacher from the school that his son had attended?"

Guy, for the third time in the last fifteen minutes, was stunned. Was it only money? That would not be a problem. Getting a divorce without any embarrassments would also not be a problem. What else might he get out of negotiating?

"How much do you want to keep that information to yourself? It's probably not worth as much as you think. The police already know that, her parents know, and the school principal is aware."

"Yes, but they are not screaming to the press. I will."

"Dad, that was my teacher."

"You keep out of this. This is between your mother and me."

"I'll give you $50,000 to sign a binding agreement not to say anything to anyone else. You give me the painting. Go back to your apartment and bring it here in two hours and I will have a certified check for you and a contract for you to sign."

"And you will also put into the contract that I am now the only owner of the two apartments in this building. I want that to be a separate agreement. I don't want to be accused of possible blackmail at a later date."

Guy nodded in agreement while realizing at the same time this price was too expensive. If he divorced, he would need cash to keep the business running, having no intention to ever agree to the proposal.

"I'll do it. It will take the rest of the day to get the papers drawn up. Come back tomorrow morning at eleven. We both can sign. It should take about a week for the full check to be ready. Come back tomorrow morning and I can give you three thousand in cash."

"Edwin, go with your mother to get the painting."

"No need to do that. I will bring it with me in the morning."

Guy thought to himself, *I'm glad you think so. I know better.*

"Edwin, let's plan on spending this evening at home. Can you prepare our favorite dish? Order something from that place we always get our fish from. the Santa Monica Seafood Market. You can decide if you want to prepare clams or mussels or even some fish. Whatever suits your fancy. I need to go out now and see my lawyer so we can get all this paperwork started and go to the bank to get the cash for her."

Edwin knew when his father was hiding things from him. He didn't know what they were, but he did think it was quite unusual for him to want to have a meal at home. The cooking request was not unusual but eating together struck him as atypical and surprising.

CHAPTER 45

Three Siblings in a Boat

"Edward, you won't believe this. But we may not have to do anything about damaging our father's reputation."

"Please don't tell me you changed your mind."

"No, mom has threated to expose Guy's affair with a schoolteacher. He is giving her the two condos to keep her mouth shut and—"

"That's not exposing him."

"I know but listen. They are both untrustworthy. I doubt if he is going to give her the apartments and I doubt if she is going to keep her mouth shut. I'm already suspicious. He's asked me to spend a night with him dining together. He never does that, so I know he is planning something. We just have to wait to see who breaks the agreement if there is ever going to be one."

"When is this agreement supposed to begin?"

"She's coming over tomorrow at eleven. I'll call you as soon as I can after it's done."

"If it's not done and your mom keeps her yap shut, that means you are a threat to him to go to the press. He might also try and ensure that you don't get the chance to do that. I'm worried for you."

"Well, let's wait and see. You also now know, and you can go to the press."

"The word of a disgruntled, alienated son is not going to carry much weight in the halls of public opinion. It's not a story that will get attention beyond a day."

"You're right. I didn't think of that. I knew there would be an advantage to having an older brother. I'll call you in the morning after the contracts are signed and if not, I'll just have to play it by ear. Have you told my sister about me?"

"Yes, Edna smiled when I told her, but she didn't have any questions. I'm not sure what she understands."

"I'm in the same boat with her. I'm not sure I understand how this all happened or where it is going."

"I guess that boat has to hold three siblings."

"Yes, but I feel that now we have two strong rowers."

CHAPTER 46

A Cuppa Coffee

"Boss, I just got this call. Roy's wife was found dead in her apartment by the cleaning lady this morning when she arrived at ten."

"Let's move, Pat. Call the crime scene lab and call the manager and the local beat cop and tell them to not touch anything. They are also to stand in front of her door until we get there, and above all, to not let anyone else in. You can make those calls while I drive."

"I'm on it, boss. You drive, I call."

The manager and the cop and the cleaning lady were waiting. So was Mr. Tapper. The cleaning lady was sobbing and muttering how nice and how generous Mrs. Roy had been. Pat took her aside and began comforting her in Spanish. Zuma told Tapper he could call the school and tell them he was going to be late. "I'll need to be asking you some questions. So just sit down and wait till Vasquez and I go through the apartment." The beat cop introduced himself as Officer Delaney and gave Zuma the key.

"After I got the call, Detective Zuma, that guy was coming out of the apartment. I told him he had to wait until you got here."

"You did good, Delaney. Did he say anything to you?"

"He said that he had come to talk with her and after hearing no response to his bell-ringing, he tried the door and it was open. He went in and saw the body slumped in a chair. He decided he'd better leave, and I ran into him as he was leaving the condo."

"Did you ask the cleaning woman if she was the only one with a key?"

"I did, and she said that Mr. Roy also has one."

"Do we have security cameras on everyone who entered the building in the last twenty-four hours?"

"There are security cameras outside and a full-time security person at the desk."

"They probably won't help but let's get a look at the digital stuff they do have. We'll be able to narrow down the search once we establish the time of death of the victim. Now, let's see what security there is inside the apartment. But first we need to take a look at the body. Delaney, wait outside with Mr. Tapper."

By this time Pat had returned and the two of them entered the kitchen. Mrs. Roy was slumped over the kitchen table. Her head was right next to a coffee cup that still had some coffee in it. A second cup with just a few drops of coffee, a half-eaten bagel with cream cheese was on a plate. The bullet had gone straight into her head from the rear of her skull. There were hair burns, which meant the weapon, had been fired at close range. There was blood spattering over the table and some of the chairs.

"Boss, it looks like nothing was touched or taken. There was a picture on the wall that looks like it has just been removed. The putty on the floor looks fresh. I wonder if that was for the hobo painting. That painting is becoming more and more famous."

"The killer knew her and was chummy enough so that they were probably sitting together. I don't think there will be any prints. I'm sure that we will not find a weapon. We need to get the bullet extracted so we can run ballistics. Take the bagel and let's see if there is any DNA that we find. Ditto for the two cups. Call Roy. If he is home, it will take him ten to fifteen minutes. Tell him I want to see him in his wife's condo. I'll speak to Tapper outside."

"Mr. Tapper, what were you planning to do at Mrs. Roy's apartment? And what time did you arrive here?"

"She had called me back shortly after I told her the date of the fundraiser. I think it was the next day. She said she had some ideas she wanted to discuss with me and wanted me to come over to her condo. She asked me to show up around ten and that she would have coffee ready. It was something about a photography book. She wanted to work out an arrangement whereby proceeds from the sales would go to her and to a parent from the school whom she was working with."

"Is the book finished?"

"No, that is one of the things she wanted to discuss with me."

"Which parent was that, Mr. Tapper?"

"It was the mother who had lost her husband. Your wife works with her child, Lucy."

CHAPTER 47

Cremation

"Oh my god. Who could have done this? Why would anyone want to kill Edna?"

"That's what we wanted to ask you, Mr. Roy."

"I have no idea. She was liked by so many. I don't think she had any enemies."

"You don't have to have enemies to have someone want to murder you. Murders are usually between people who know each other well." Zuma paused and gazed intently at Roy. "Who will gain from her death, Mr. Roy?"

"Detective Zuma, you know I will but that doesn't mean I would want her dead or want to murder her."

"When was your last contact with her?"

"Yesterday morning. She had gotten another hobo painting from Claudia Berlin and she was going to sell it to me."

"Can you tell me how much she was asking?"

"Detective, you and I have been here before. Those are personal questions you are asking and unless you charge me, I am not going to answer your questions."

"So, you are not in possession of the painting that was taken from your wife's condo?"

"No, but I wish I was."

"Mr. Roy, after we do a thorough search of the crime scene, we are going to have to take your wife's body down for a physical examination. We're going to extract the bullet to get ballistics. That's going to take a few days. It's not a great time to ask but do you have any wishes for how you would like us to handle the body after we do a physical?"

"Cremate it. I don't believe in ceremonies or supporting the funeral business."

"Mr. Roy, would you take a closer look at the coffee cups on the table? Have you seen them before? Are they familiar?"

"They look like ones I picked up for Edna in Thailand?"

"Can you check that?"

"Can I pick up the cup?"

"Sure."

"Well, here it is, made in Thailand."

"Thank you, Mr. Roy. Officer Delaney would you please take the food and plates down to our lab and escort Mr. Roy out."

"No problem, Detective."

"Detective Zuma, you have my fingerprints on the cup you just asked me to pick up. I don't want to be framed. I want it noted in front of your two assistants that you asked me to do this."

"Sure, I'll put it in an e-mail when I get back to the office."

"I want the e-mail now. Can you do that, please?"

"I'll do it when I get back to my office."

"I'm not going to leave. I'm calling my lawyer right now."

Zuma smiled. This guy didn't miss a beat. After a minute on the phone with his lawyer, Mr. Roy left.

"Boss, this guy is like a bee in a flower patch. He buzzes all around going into whatever flower he selects, sucks the nectar out, and leaves with no trace. And I don't think he was too upset with his wife's murder or even too surprised."

"Yes, Pat, but he does not lose his stinger when he commits murder. First, a teacher, then an art collector, and now a wife. The man doesn't run out of stingers. Let *me* do the body evaluation, and you examine the digital recordings for visuals while we wait for ballistics."

"If you're thinking what I'm thinking, the ballistics and weapon will match the Truro murder."

"I agree, Pat. At this point, it is not likely to be Guy and more likely to be someone who works for him or is under his control. But we need to bring him in and have him sweat. That's why I did that little thing with the coffee cup. I want him to know we also don't miss a beat and that he is a suspect. I want him nervous. He needs to account for all his whereabouts. And we need to figure out how someone could have gotten into Mrs. Roy's condo, sat with her while she was eating, and managed to stand up, walk behind her, quickly pull out a gun, put a bullet into her skull, and left with a painting."

"Getting in must have been easy. She knew the person well enough to serve them coffee. Getting out with the painting must have been more challenging. I'll check with desk security and get all the digital records in the house."

CHAPTER 48

Banners, Uniforms, and Trophies

There was a decorative unfurled banner at the top of the store. Guy Roy's name and picture was in one of the windows along with pictures of him smiling and giving out trophies to happy high school students. After Pat introduced himself, he asked the manager how long he had been working at the store.

"I have been working here as a manager for five years. Yes, I am paid well, well enough to support a family, and I now have three kids. Mr. Roy wants continuity, and he has promised that if I stay on, he will pay for my kids' private school. He also knows that the employees and the students we hire like me."

"Is there anything you can tell me about the students?"

"Well, they certainly come from the side of the tracks that I didn't come from."

"So why do you think they want to work here?"

"It's a chance for them to meet students from other schools. The guys like it because they meet girls who come in to buy soccer, track, volleyball, and basketball gear—that's a lot of girls. We don't have any gals selling but that's not because we discriminate. We had a few but the guys tended to give them the cold shoulder. It changed the way they could talk about the girls who were coming in and they didn't like it."

"Are there anything like bonuses or rewards for doing well?"

"I'm not sure what you mean. They all get extra cash at Christmas if they have worked here for the entire year."

"So, there are no rewards or commissions to the top sellers?"

"No, we have a pretty steady business. They really can't sell extra uniforms or trophies. A team usually needs the same number of uniforms every year."

"So aside from the opportunity to meet girls, is there any other reason you think they might be working here."

"I don't know. I've often wondered about that myself. When I have asked, they usually say they like working with students from other schools and meeting kids their own age. The kids who do our selling come from different schools. We try to have at least one kid from each school on the floor at any one time."

"And how many schools do you represent?"

"We have six fairly large schools and a few very small private schools. Roy lets me do the interviews and the hiring for the small schools. They are not a big part of the business."

"Oh, so Mr. Roy does the hiring for these other bigger schools?"

"Yes. I'm not sure how he does it. They just show up here after he gives me their names and I train them. He has never been wrong in his selections. It must be the years he's been in business."

"Well, thank you very much for your help. I wish you luck with your family. Would you mind introducing me to one of the kids that Roy hired and that you have working on the floor now?"

"Sure, no problem. The one over there talking is from a big school."

The boy was not intimidated when Detective Pat Vasquez flashed his badge. Pat realized that even though the young man was probably only sixteen, he had already learned his place in the world was not going to be tarnished by questioning from those who were inferior.

He left with a touch of anger believing that most of the kids already knew they were members in a privileged club. They were going to be the future brutes of the world. They would have gloves so there would be no scars or marks, but they were going to be hiring and firing, building apartment buildings, taking away land,

and donating money to charity while voting against high wages or affordable housing. The hiring image made him realize that Roy's hiring practices could be an important clue to his nefarious activities. Before he stepped into his car, he turned around and looked at the sign and the storefront. There was the brightness with so many different colors representing the schools and the sun reflecting off the golden trophies. It was amazing that something so rich in hues could cover and hide murkiness.

CHAPTER 49

A World-Famous Chair

Sonia was pleased to see how well Lucy had been doing despite the loss of Hope. Claudia, the new teacher, had quickly been adopted by Lucy and hardly a day had passed that Lucy wouldn't come home excited about something that she had learned or how Claudia had complemented her or shown her work to others in the class. As she was waiting to pick Lucy up from school and thinking of what she could provide for the school's next fundraiser, Lucy bounced into her car.

"Mrs. Berlin, Claudia, told the class that the new teachers who teach German were going to take eight children to visit Germany and see the museums. Mommy, can I go to Germany?"

Sonia did all she could to stop from laughing out loud. She knew Lucy had no idea where Germany was. Sonia was taken aback, partly by the request but also by Lucy's exuberance.

"I need to find out more about it. Who is going and how long will it be for?"

Sonia was surprised at her willingness to entertain the possibility that Lucy would be gone from her home. She had often fretted about any overnights that Lucy had taken. The fact that Lucy was willing to go was a sign that perhaps her abandonment issue had faded and that she was now willing to venture into the world without fear. She realized also that it might be hard for her to let her go. Who was it exactly who had the abandonment issue? She had an epiphany and realized how alone she was, how angry she had been to get rid of her husband, and how badly and disgusted she felt that his body was rotting in a piece of furniture that she had made. Had she made a mistake? Had her rage blinded her to all the implications of the loss of a husband and a father to her daughter? She shuddered. Her thoughts returned to the school and Lucy. She needed to still be very careful around Claudia and the detective. She knew he was not going to give up.

"It will take me a few days, but if it is possible, sweetheart. I would be happy to let you do this. Lucy, I'm going to design some furniture for the next fundraiser from your school. I'm thinking of two chairs. When we go home, let me show you some models of chairs made by a famous person. His name is Herman Miller. I'm thinking about how to change them. Would you like to help me draw up some models that would be different?"

"Sure, Mommy, you know how much I love to work with you."

Sonia thought that if she gave the school two chairs and sold them as a package, she would give half the proceeds to the school and keep the other half. If Lucy were going to go to Germany, this would help pay for the trip. She wondered if Claudia would be going on the trip with the other teachers. Maybe a parent from the school had to accompany the couple. Two adults with eight kids would be a lot to handle. She thought of herself but quickly rejected that idea. That would not be in Lucy's best interests nor in hers.

"Sweetheart, lets pick up some drawing paper and some softwood so you can carve models of a world-famous chair."

CHAPTER 50

A Home Is Removed

"Boss, this woman, I think she is homeless, has been waiting for you for six hours. She insists on speaking with you and only you. I haven't been able to get her to tell me what it about."

"Pat, bring her in and stay with me."

Zuma saw a somewhat attractive woman walk gracefully into his office. He guessed her age to be about fifty. She had a kind face but very worn clothing. He motioned to have her take a seat.

"Detective Zuma, I am here to ask you for your help. The reason I want to speak with only you has to do with the way I have seen you conduct yourself on the bluffs with the other homeless people. I am one of them."

Zuma perked up. Any information about the bluffs and the homeless and the paintings alerted him.

"How can I help you, Ms....?"

"My name is Mary Follette. I have been homeless for about three months. I was in arrears in my rent and when the government shutdown came, I didn't receive my check. I couldn't pay the rent. The landlord wouldn't give me another extension. He knew I was eventually going to get paid, but he saw the opportunity to raise the rent on the rent-controlled apartments."

Zuma waited patiently. He didn't think that Mary Follette was going to ask for a loan.

"As I said, I have been homeless but have been living out of my car. In the mornings, I use the bathrooms either on the bluffs or in a gas station to wash up and change my clothes. After I dress, I look for a job."

"What kind of work do you do?"

"I'm a clerk, stenographer, but can do any number of things. I've had a lot of jobs. Yesterday, I was prepared to seek another job. When I came out of a gas station that I had never used before to put my gear back into the car, it was gone. At first, I thought it was stolen but realized that nobody would want a car that was filled with stuff and clothing. After a while, I noticed that I had parked in a tow-away zone. I couldn't walk into the office applying for a job with my bag of clothing and I was panicky about my car. It is my home. I walked all the way to the place in West LA, where they keep the towed cars. I think it is called Quick Silver. They said I needed to pay them $293.00 to get my car back. My pleadings were to no avail. If I can't get the car, I have no place to sleep. It is too dangerous for a woman to be sleeping in a doorway and besides, I have no extra clothing. I need to get my home back."

"What do you think I can do?"

"Can you call Quick Silver and tell them you need the car for some unsolved crime? Can you call them and tell them to release the car to me, as you need me to help you on a case? I don't know what you can do or are willing to do. I know you are a kind man and a good man. If you put out the money, I will pay you back in full. You have my word."

Zuma reflected back on the Band-Aid discussion he had earlier with the principal at SurePaths. Here it was another Band-Aid problem. Homelessness was not going to be solved by any individual act of human kindness, but this woman was obviously decent and ambitious and had fallen off the grid not because of anything she had done. After a moment, he thought he could provide a Band-Aid.

"I could make a requisition to get your car back as we need it to continue an investigation. If they want money, I will either lay it out or ask Detective Vasquez to figure out a way that the department can pay for the release. Pat, can you do that? We have to provide some paperwork that would argue for the inspection or use of this car as to which crime we are pursuing. We can indicate that it is related it to the theft of the paintings or drug selling. I'll get on it right away, Ms. Follette. Detective Vasquez can give you a lift back to Quick Silver as soon as the paperwork is completed. You should have your home back by this evening."

"Thank you, Detectives."

"Ms. Follette, since there is something legitimate about requesting your car, I am going to ask you to help us out in gathering some information."

"I'll do whatever you ask, Detective Zuma."

Zuma took out a charcoal picture of the hobo that Claudia had made.

"Do you recognize this man?"

"I do, Detective. He is one of the least aggressive men on the bluffs. He probably has some mental illness. He and I are friendly."

"What do you mean by 'friendly?'"

"Oh, it's not romantic. But he has invited me into a place that he has. It's a small apartment that is furnished pretty nicely. It's nicer than any other homeless men I know. The way I see it, he doesn't have to be homeless, but I don't ask him questions. He doesn't have to come out to the bluffs from his nice apartment dressed in his homeless garb, but he does it. I figured it was a way for him to feel free."

"He has a brother. And we are trying to figure out what exactly the relationship is about. Your friend also sells drugs to other homeless folks and some of the straight people, and we want to know where he gets his drugs."

"We're not that close. And if I were to ask him personal questions, he would clam up and not talk to me anymore."

"I don't want you to ask questions. I want you to wait and just develop the relationship. If it doesn't lead anywhere, that's okay. If it does, it might help us a great deal. Are you willing to try? I don't think you have anything to lose."

"Yes."

"Good. Thank you for your willingness. Here are numbers to call Detective Vasquez or me directly."

"Blessings to both of you."

"Now, just go in the other room while Detective Vasquez draws up the paperwork and you should be able to have your home back by this evening."

Zuma thought that Claudia would be proud of him. Zuma also knew it was just another Band-Aid.

CHAPTER 51

Photography and Furniture

Even though she recognized her through the peephole, Sonia was surprised to see Edna Roy standing in the doorway.

"Please, come in. I think I met you at the last fundraiser and you bought the painting. I also remember that you said you admired my furniture and that if you had more money that you would be eager to purchase something of mine."

Edna was impressed with the graceful way that Sonia got right down to business. She thought her proposal might work out to be financially lucrative for both of them.

"Yes, I am here to see if there is something you will make for me that I will purchase and I'm also here to propose a business arrangement."

"Let's talk about the proposal after I hear what you are interested in buying. May I assume that you have been able to come into more money?"

Edna was impressed again with the directness and focus that Sonia had for selling her work.

"Yes, I have money now or at least I will have it in a day or two. I'd like to order two of the same pieces you made for the fundraiser, but they would have to be smaller...I imagine about half the size would fit nicely into my condo."

"Mrs. Roy, my reputation has been built around making big pieces. I am not sure it's a good idea that I should venture to change that. The smaller piece would cost you almost as much as the larger ones."

"Please, call me Edna, and I would like to call you Sonia. I would like you to consider that a change might help you. I am asking for something similar but much smaller and with different woods. This will be a piece that is bolder in its statement. It would make the owners of your larger pieces feel special and perhaps even increase their value, since you have stopped making them. You could even offer to buy them back at a reduced price if they so wish."

"I'll only agree to consider making the pieces for you if you do not advertise them or put them on some social media platform."

"Good. I will assume that the price for these two will be the same as the larger ones you produced for the fundraiser."

"No, they will be more expensive. There is more labor involved with fitting smaller piece of different woods together and gluing them so that there is absolutely no space between them. I can't give you an exact price, but I would think it's at least 20 percent more. If it's less, I will charge you less. I can't imagine it would be more than 20 percent."

"Okay, here is $500 as a down payment. Would it be possible for me to select the woods?"

"That would take too much time as I would have to keep coordinating my work schedule with your schedule. You will just have to leave it up to me."

The woman was all business. She saw no need to hesitate and proceeded with her proposal.

"Sonia, you may know I'm a photographer. I would like to do a book of still lifes. Nature and man-made or in your case, woman-made. It would be a coffee table book. I already have a good reputation, and I would like to make a proposal to a publisher who likes my work. Your work on any of the pieces you have made or will be making would be the only person created still life in the book. It is a way for you to get better known and probably create more business for you. I propose that we would split royalties on the book and that I take 10 percent of any sales that you get from the book."

Sonia hesitated. Would the increase in work created a pace that she was trying to avoid? Would it take time away from Lucy? The money would be wonderful and maybe she could hire a helper to do some of the labor involved in the making of furniture.

"I'm willing to try it as long as you understand that I am not on any time pressure to produce anything for a client. They will just have to wait."

Edna laughed. "Waiting will make them feel they are getting something even more precious."

"I'm making two chairs for the fundraiser. I think putting them into your book would be a plus for you and me. I have a four-poster bed that I use that would also fit in. Maybe you want to fly up to Vancouver and see those big pieces and how they are being used. That might make it also special for the book. I don't think any more that two of anything should be in there."

"Great idea, Sonia. I'll just put that down as expenses for the production of our work."

Sonia decided to pry a bit. "I'm surprised that you are into making money through your photography. I had the impression at the fundraiser that your payment for the painting meant you and your husband were comfortable."

"Oh, yes we are comfortable with money. But at this point, there is very little in our marriage that is comfortable."

Sonia decided that was an invitation to probe more. "Oh, I'm sorry to hear that. Are the two of you divorcing?"

"Yes, I think so. It will be a very expensive divorce for him. He has done what the books say all or most men do. Its classic and predictable."

"You don't have to tell me what that is. I had the same experience. You seem amazingly calm for someone whose husband has cheated on her. I was not calm. I was anything but calm. I wanted to murder him from the moment I found out."

She immediately regretted this last uttering.

"Of course, I never even got the chance. The bastard just left."

Edna laughed. "Well, murdering him is still an option. But at this point, I think I can squeeze a fortune out of him by not going to court. In that way, he can keep his squeaky-clean image of a philanthropist and successful businessman. I will make him pay for that. How did you make your husband pay? What methods had you considered?"

It was Sonia's turn to laugh. She impulsively pointed to the large chest of drawers that was unpainted in the corner.

Edna roared, "Now that's putting your work to a very worthwhile use. You'd only have to worry about the smell. I'm sure that was the least of the problems you had."

Sonia stopped. Hadn't she just admitted to doing away with her husband? She tried to recoup.

"He already smelled bad from not taking a shower every day. And our marriage had stunk for a long time."

It was Edna's turn to be cool. "Well, if I ever decide to do the deed, I will call upon you for a large chest of drawers. Right now, we have a business arrangement. I can have a contract drawn up and bring it to you in a day or so. Would that be okay?"

"That would be fine. Give me a call before you come. It's best if you come early in the morning after I get Lucy off to school and before I start to work."

Sonia sat down. She had to think. Could she trust Edna with what she had said? It wasn't anything directly about the murder of her husband, but it could be important in a legal trial. She was worried that ongoing business contacts with Edna would also remind her that Edna had indirect knowledge. Was this any more difficult than Zuma and his suspicions? She felt that it would be since Zuma was not around that much. She realized and decided that she would not want Edna to be around that much either.

CHAPTER 52

Hobos and Garbage

Edna was surprised to get the knock at such an early hour. Looking through the peephole, she saw Sonia.

"I thought about your proposal. Before you solidify the contract, I'd like to go over a few more details. This shouldn't take long."

"Sit down. Let me make you a cup of coffee."

When Edna sat her coffee down, Sonia got up and indicated she would need sweetener. As she walked towards the counter past Edna, Sonia passed directly in back of her, turned around, removed the revolver, pointed it at the nape of her neck, raised it to a forty-five-degree angle, and pulled the trigger. She died instantly and there was a large splattering of blood on the coffee cups, the table, and the chairs. She knew it would make the police suspicious if the hobo painting was gone and so she took it off the wall. She had brought the same kind of tape and plastic that she had used after she had murdered her husband. She rolled the painting up in a hollow tube. When she left the apartment, the tube was hidden in her coat. It would look too suspicious if she walked out with the bulge in her coat, but she had prepared for that. She dropped it down the garbage shaft that was at the end of the hallway. Now it would be just a matter to convince the police that she found Mrs. Roy already dead. As she waited for the elevator, she thought that a good painting was going to end up in a garbage heap. That's where real hobos end up in our society. Art is safe in museums. Hobos are not safe in this world.

CHAPTER 53

Respecting Artists

Zuma was facing the woman he believed had already committed one murder. Now it looked like this would be her second. He was hoping for a better outcome.

"Let's go over this again. You arrived at Mrs. Roy's condo in order to discuss the details of a contract that you had spoken about earlier. And the contract was about a book that you and she were going to produce. You arrived there at about 9:10 or so, knocked on the door, and when there was no answer you went in and saw her body. You checked it and felt no pulse and you immediately went downstairs to speak to security. Why didn't you call the police?"

"I was frazzled, Detective Zuma. I'm sure you know that I'm not as accustomed to see corpses as you are."

"Did you notice anything about the apartment? Were things in disarray? Did you notice that a painting had been taken off the wall?"

"No, as I said I was upset. It was gruesome. There was blood all over the table and chairs.

How do you know it was 9:10 when you arrived?"

"You can check the security camera in the building. As I was looking for a pulse, I also noticed the time on the clock on her wall."

"Will there be fingerprints on Mrs. Roy's neck where you checked her pulse? I assume that's where you touched her."

"Yes, there should be. Detective, how much longer will you need me to be here? I need to pick up my daughter. I have told you everything I know."

"Just a few minutes more. Do you have a copy of the contract? Can you tell me what the contract was about? Roughly, that is."

"She and I were going to do a coffee table book on still lifes. I would be letting her take photos of my furniture and she was going to provide shots of animal life that she had taken all around Santa Monica."

"What do you mean animal life?"

"The birds on the beach and bluffs, cats and dogs on leashes or running wild."

"Did you ever see the contract?"

"No, that was something she was going to have her lawyer draw up in the next day or so. I wanted to speak to her before she went ahead and would have to pay her lawyer for his time. I never saw it because I don't think it ever got done."

"What didn't you like about the arrangement that you had worked out?"

"I didn't think it would be to my advantage to make smaller pieces of furniture. She had convinced me otherwise, but I changed my mind."

"Why couldn't you just call her and tell her that?"

"I liked her and respected her as a photographer and thought she deserved an explanation that would go over better person to person. We're both artists, and it's not often that we get respect from the world. We can, at least, respect each other."

Zuma had heard similar words from Claudia. He shuddered as he thought of the two women as alike while also realizing they were radically different.

CHAPTER 54

Working the Edges

"Pat, it's drawing board time."

"I can tell that's what you were thinking, boss. Your toothpick is out and you are humming that tune. I think it's 'Blowin in the Wind.'"

"Good for you, Pat. I know there were a lot of songs to choose from. He was prolific. So, let's see what's 'blowin' in the wind.'"

"Okay, boss. Let me put the four vics on the board. Next to each one I will list possible and more-likely suspects. First one is roommate? Boyfriend of roommate still likely. No one else as a possible perp."

"I would still not rule that out. If it is someone they are connected to the school and to Hope."

"Teacher? Guy is the most likely. Other possibilities are other teachers, the principal, or even a parent."

"Truro art dealer? Son of Guy. Brother of Guy or hired gun."

"Mrs. Roy? Furniture maker or Tapper. Mr. Roy has good alibi."

"Stolen items are hobo painting from Truro and from Mr. Guy Roy's apartment. The suspects are son of Guy, brother of Guy, or furniture maker."

"No one shows up as likely on all four vics."

We're probably dealing with more than one murderer."

"I think your right, Pat. Let's just put aside the Truro murder. Let's just focus on Mrs. Roy. I think if we can pin that one down, we'll get confessions or better leads to the others."

"What does the digital show on the condo?"

"It confirms what the two suspects said about timing. There were no prints, except for Roy's on the cup and the lady furniture maker's on the neck. A painting had just been removed and there were no prints on the wall. I think it must be, by now, the most famous painting in Santa Monica or at least the one that everyone wants to own."

"Pat, we're dealing with someone who is meticulous. The most meticulous of our suspects is our furniture lady. Let's think again what her motives might be. What would she have to gain by murdering Edna Roy? Why would she take a painting and where is it? If we're not trying to be as meticulous as she is, we're not going to find anything out. Suppose the reason for the murder had nothing to do with money, sex, or power."

"What else might it be?"

"The lady was hiding her husband's murder from me, right? Maybe Edna had found something out about the murder and Sonia became afraid."

"Okay, that gives us a motive. We have a body but no weapon. And ballistics does not match the weapon that was used in Truro."

"I think we need to go back and work around the edges. We need to do the following. What have the Schnables discovered? What is going on with Tapper? Let's call him in again. We need to find out if anything is going on with the Roy children and what is going on with Roy's brother. Who is the most likely of our suspects who would want the hobo painting? I can't imagine anyone but Roy wanting it. Let's figure out how he may have gotten hold of it or who might be holding it for him. Let's get a court order to look at Roy's income tax records for the past three years. And while I'm thinking tax records, let's get Tapper's. For now, let's call it a day. We're not in a car chase. The murderers are not leaving town."

Zuma pulled up to his home. He was leaving the edges to get to the heart of his heart. Claudia greeted him with a big smile, a long hug, and the edges just faded away as he nestled into the center of his world.

CHAPTER 55

A Most Eligible Bachelor

Roy felt smug. Edna would no longer be seeking a divorce and the threat to ruin his reputation had been removed. He knew that they were going to try and pin her murder on him, but he also knew that since he hadn't done it that he would not be going to trial. There had been no follow up on the Truro murder, so he believed that the investigation had come to a dead end.

The affair with Hope had ended badly, but it did not seem that any more investigation was going to occur. Maybe that would be another dead end.

Were there any loose ends with Carl? Were there things about his sons that he had to worry about? His smugness increased. He would now be able to look for a new girlfriend and make sure the banner and toy business were doing well with their selling of drugs. He was looking forward to the next fundraiser where he would be showing up as a widower with a good tan, fine suit, and able to purchase any items that he like. He realized that the hobo painting was missing but no longer felt that anyone connecting the character in the painting as his brother was as threatening as it had seemed before. He realized that supplying Carl with drugs was a risk and that could be traced back to him and began having second thoughts about it. Maybe it would be good to have him stop. He could just give him some money every week or so that he could use as he saw fit. He fancied himself as a most eligible bachelor.

CHAPTER 56

A Therapist Observes

"Dr. Milgram, I need a consult from you. I'm calling in a suspect and I want you to be in our observation room. He will show up with a lawyer. He's a pretty cool customer. Without trying to prejudice you about the case in advance, could you clear your calendar if I gave you a few days' notice?"

"No problem. I'll only need two days to alert my patients. Just tell me when, Detective Zuma. I'm always eager to help. Are you sure you want me to just do an observation?"

"Therapy would be better, of course, but there is no reason that I could present to him so that he might agree to see you for therapy. I'm going to call him now and I'll call you right back to let you know if and when he is coming in so you can do the observation."

"Mr. Roy? This is Detective Zuma. I'm going to ask your cooperation. I would like you to come down for an interview. No, I'm not charging you with anything. I know you have told me everything about your wife and brother, your marriages and children, and Hope, but there are a few issues that I'm just not clear about. Yes, of course, you can bring your lawyer. Would Thursday afternoon work for you? How long? Probably no more than one and a half hours. Thank you for your willingness to do this."

Roy roared to himself when he got off the phone. That is a Columbo move he thought. Peter Falk would be proud. He knew that Zuma was not at all unclear about any of the things that he had told him about. This was an obvious effort to trap him. He would cooperate but not as a cooperative witness. He would cooperate by listening to his lawyer's advice about any questions. He also knew that his lawyer would advise him to not answer any questions on the grounds of self-incrimination.

Zuma, Pat, and a stenographer who was using a recorder, which Roy had agreed to, sat facing Roy and his lawyer. After a brief introduction of all parties present, the questioning began. Zuma, without notes, went over Roy's whereabouts on the dates the vics were murdered. Roy affirmed the names of witnesses who could verify his stories in each of these cases. Zuma asked Roy whether he knew any of the people who might have killed Hope Schnable, Roy's first or second wife, and a murdered man in Truro. Roy answered no to all of these. He was not breaking a sweat. When Zuma asked him directly if he had killed any of the same people, the lawyer advised him not to answer. "Under advisement of my lawyer, Detective Zuma, I refuse to answer any of those questions."

"Mr. Roy, can you let us know about your feelings for some of the people in your life, like your children?"

"Detective Zuma, that is not a question that has relevance for your purpose of investigating a murder case. I urge my client to be nonresponsive."

"Thank you, counsel. I have nothing to hide. Let me answer."

For the next ten minutes Roy responded to Zuma's questions about his children, his two wives, and his lover. Zuma had to direct him to talk about his feelings as opposed to the information that Roy kept providing.

When he finished, Zuma thank Roy for coming in. "You have been helpful."

After he exited, Roy laughed. He believed it was a waste of Zuma's time. He knew Zuma was cagey and would expect him not to help, so why had he called him in? He had provided no new information. Had he been helpful? He didn't believe he had but he also hoped not.

Zuma was pleased with the interview. He was very patient as Roy answered with details that Zuma had provided earlier. He displayed no difference in tone or eagerness when he got to the questions that he had hoped would allow Milgram to assess Roy's character.

"Okay, Dr. Milgram, what did you see?"

"You have one tough cookie on your hands. He is an original. Definitely a man of steel. I would say he is a first-class sociopath."

"Tell me what that means to you, Dr. Milgram. When did you see it in the interview?"

"His feelings about children, lover, wives, and brother were about him and what they did to him. He could not access any feelings of tenderness, remorse, or regrets. He is incapable of seeing that he can hurt or harm others."

"So, do you think he was lying?"

"I think he is incapable of telling the truth about his actions if it is suggested that they are immoral or illegal. Others don't exist as independent of him or his ego. If you tell him as you did, that perhaps his children felt abandoned, he pointed out how he had helped them. He will justify any action he has committed no matter what it is."

"Even murder?

"Yes, even murder. When you asked him about his favorite activities, he expressed no pleasure in the activity. The running and the gym workouts were described as making him fit and strong and powerful."

"How did you interpret his response to the hypothetical situation you gave him with the father hitting the child?

"It was consistent with what I assess his character to be. He had no empathy for the child who was being beaten. Most people do not want to interfere with a parent disciplining a child. But they usually feel bad for the child and cite the rule about parents' right to discipline. Or they seek to interfere indirectly with the beating, even if they are frightened, by going to the police. The healthy ones don't cite the rule and just seek to stop it. He said the parent had a right to discipline. He did not register any pain for the child."

"And that he cited parents' right to discipline told you what?"

"That he is rigid and that he lacks empathy."

"Thank you, Dr. Milgram. I'm not sure how I can use this, but it makes it clearer to Pat and me what we are dealing with. If we ever get to court, I will be calling on you again."

"Of course, Detective. At your service, always."

"Pat, did Milgram's' description feel right to you?"

"Yes, boss. He put into words what I had been feeling about this creep but could not verbalize. We'll never be able to catch him in a lie, but I think Milgram nailed him."

"Well, let's hope we can do the same."

"We will, boss. This creep will soon be regretting that he was so cooperative."

"Remember, Pat, he is incapable of feeling regret. He will turn it all on us."

"When he does that, at lease we'll know there is fear buried somewhere in his steely soul."

CHAPTER 57

The Hobo and the Homeless

Walking on the bluffs in the morning and seeing her old homeless buddy on the bluffs made Mary Follette smile. Carl lit up when he saw her.

"Would you like to share some of my latte, Mary?"

"No thanks, Carl, but I am happy to see that you are in a good mood."

Good moods had not been frequent occurrences in their encounters. Sometimes, Carl was sullen while at other times he ignored her completely. She assumed that this was part of his mental illness.

"I am in a good mood and am happy to see you. We have known each other for a long time and have shared these bluffs with so many others who are no longer here, but we have survived. We are the strong ones."

"Yes, we have shared homelessness, a lack of clothing, hunger, drugs, arrests, and now we share something else."

"What is that?"

"A detective. Detective Zuma."

His smile changed, and a look of suspicion emerged.

"What have you been doing with him? What has he said about me?"

"Let's sit down. It's a long story. If we sit near the bathroom no one will bother us."

After recounting her story about the impounded vehicle and her begging Zuma for help, she told him about the detective's request.

"So, he wants you to keep an eye on me?"

"I think he wants to know how you are scoring drugs and who the regular straights are as well as your whereabouts. He would really like to make the bluffs a place where citizens would not be bothered by us and also unable to buy drugs. He also mentioned something about a painting of yours that has been lost. I think he said there was more than one painting."

"So, Mary what are you going to do for our detective in common?"

"That's why I'm glad I ran into you. Zuma is a nice guy, but I have no future even now that my car has been returned. I need to make some money, to clean up, apply for jobs, and provide an employer with a legitimate address so no one thinks I'm homeless."

"How do I fit in with those plans?"

"I thought I could tell Zuma that you are no longer dealing and that you are totally dependent on begging. I could get drugs for us, and with my car, we could travel around the city and sell. We split money fifty-fifty after costs and my gas. We need to clean up before we go out and sell."

"Don't you feel bad lying after he helped you?"

"Not as bad as I would feel if I was stuck and didn't see a way out of here, which I don't. I need to get money so I can get a job, so I can earn money and stop living in my car."

"I can help you with an address right now, if you like. We can use my place to change and keep our clothes. I have parking. We would not have to make it obvious that you are staying there or sleeping there."

Mary saw the trouble the moment he had finished. Carl was a nice guy and a bit unstable, but mostly, he was a man.

"Let's hold off on the sleeping arrangements. I appreciate the address and the place to wash and change clothes. I think I had better continue sleeping in my car to prevent Zuma from getting suspicious about my new source of income. You're going to have to spend a few days not selling and just begging. I think Zuma will check on my story."

"When do we start?"

"We can start tomorrow morning. No one will notice that you're gone for the day. I'll have my new clothes, as you will, and I can pick you up in my car. Let's meet at nine. Northwest corner of 3rd and Broadway. Carl, can you loan me money to get some clothes? I'll pay you back with our first sales."

"Sure. Let's meet in about an hour. I'll go and get some cash. Will $100 do it?"

"I'm not sure. It's been so long since I went shopping for clothes. Make it $300. I'll give you back whatever I don't spend."

"Mary, I can get us a steady supply of drugs. How about if I do that? I can score some later today and we can meet here tomorrow morning."

"Right now, that sounds good. It's better if we switch off getting the drugs. That way we are less likely to be discovered. And what is this thing with a painting? What gives with that?"

"It's a sweet story. Let me save it for tomorrow."

Carl was surprised that Guy picked up the phone. "Guy, it's me, I want to talk to you about getting some more stuff. What do you mean you're not sure? We need to meet. Yes, I think we do. Can you run to the bluffs? I can meet you at the turnaround. How long? Okay. See you in two hours."

"Carl, I want you to stop selling. I am willing to give you $200 a week as a regular stipend. All you have to do is agree to stop selling drugs and dressing like a homeless person. You stay away from the bluffs. If the painting shows up and someone recognizes you and links the two of us together, I can talk about how I helped you and that you are now on your feet. You keep your place, which I continue to pay for. All you have to do is stop begging, stop selling, and look presentable wherever you go and whatever you do."

"What's this switch about, my dear brother?"

"I'm a widower now, a most eligible widower. I'm looking to meet a very wealthy lady, and I don't want to be seen as having any baggage in my family. If I can anticipate how I would like to be seen, I want to be perceived as the good brother."

Carl was impressed with how honest Guy could be about his less-than-honorable motives.

"Okay, we have a deal. I need $300 right away to get some new clothes." He smiled to himself, as he knew he, like his brother, had less than honorable motives.

CHAPTER 58

An Offer you Can Refuse

The spring fundraiser had a larger attendance than the one earlier in the year. The attendees all dressed formally with the fundraiser being followed by dinner and dancing. Sonia couldn't help noticing that Zuma and Claudia were a handsome couple. She was not going to be responsive to their looks or graciousness as she was eager to do business. In addition to the two chairs that she had brought for sale, there was one of her trademark pieces, a massive chest of drawers.

Zuma stayed at Claudia's side while many parents came up to her and let her know how wonderful their children found her to be and how much they enjoyed the painting and the wood working that was going on in her classroom. She was casual about introducing Joe and did not announce that he was a detective. Many of the parents knew him.

"So, Detective Zuma, we saw you a few nights ago and you were undecided about taking the Boston chief of police job. Are you any closer to making a decision? I'm sure I speak for many when I say we sure would hate to see you leave."

"Thank you for your kind words. I am no closer to deciding now than before."

In fact, Joe and Claudia had discussed the possible move. It was a big honor but thinking about how much less time he would have with Claudia, he had just about decided not to move. He knew he would be on call whenever Logan Airport was being threatened and the memory of the marathon bomber was still in all Bostonians awareness. He knew they were extra sensitive, on the lookout for suspects, and calling in lots of possible tips. His being nearer the Cape was an upside but knowing that he would be on call made the job less appealing than it might have been a few years ago, before Claudia. His boys would be proud but that was not that important to him.

Claudia had not weighed in with any thinking, as she did not want to prevent him from moving up in his career. She was relieved and happy when he had told her that he was about 97 percent sure he would not take the job. He wanted to wait till the end of the week.

"And what's the 3 percent that's holding you back from being 100 percent?"

"If I could solve these cases and see Pat taking my position, I would retire and might take it for a year. It would be a large increase in salary as well as my retirement. That would be a bundle of cash for us to fix up the house at the Cape. Also, if anything happened to you, I would want to plunge myself into a new challenge."

"You will solve the cases. That's one percent. Pat would be a good choice to replace you that's two percent. But since nothing is going to happen to me, you're stuck with one percent keeping you from going to Boston. And besides, we do not need the money to fix up the house."

"Ladies and gentlemen," Tapper was speaking, "we have had a most successful fundraiser, having raised $10,000 more than last year. Let us now retire to the outdoor tent for dinner and dancing. Those who want to have their purchases delivered, please see me with your ticket."

Sonia made it her business to say goodnight to Zuma and Claudia. All her pieces had sold, and she was not going to stay. Claudia's landscapes had also sold, and the purchasers came up to tell her how much their daughter had wanted to have one of the paintings she did.

"Honey, you teach the kids good taste and they bring pressure on their folks to exercise good taste. You are creating a body of purchasers for your work."

"It's only children."

"Yes, but they still have the eyes of the innocent. They have not been told what they should own. They know what they like. They can purchase with the best of the well-trained art connoisseurs."

During the dancing, Zuma noticed that Guy Roy had been with one woman. She had a very large diamond bracelet and a necklace to match. He thought of Roy as a well-trained hunter who silently stalked his prey, surprised them and never left a mess after killing them.

CHAPTER 59

The Hunters

Sonia had the $500 dollar deposit that Edna Roy gave her and was ambivalent about what to do with it. The chairs had sold, her big piece had sold, and by all rights, she should have given back the money, but Edna was dead. She could keep it, and no one would know. They only had a verbal agreement. She could also donate it to the school. For reasons that were unclear to her, she decided to call Guy Roy.

"Yes, your wife had given me a deposit to make the chairs. If I sold them, I was to return it, as it is rightfully hers. And I guess it should go to you."

"That's very kind of you. Is there any chance you would be able to bring the check over to my condo? I know it is in the same building that Edna was killed in, but I am on a different floor. You won't have to bypass any of the horrid scene."

"I'd like that. Will early afternoon be okay? I have to pick up my daughter later on."

The two hunters met at 1:00 PM. Sonia was impressed with the artwork and with the blue-like glassy stainless-steel quality of the place. The sun made it glitter, making it seem that there was no border between the blue of the ocean and the blueness of the condo.

Sonia replied "nothing" to Roy's inquiring about a beverage.

Roy eyed her carefully. He thought she had a good body, very strong hands, good skin, and an ample, full bosom. Her overall presentation was one of strength much like her furniture. He assessed her to be confident in bed and in her work site. He knew that he would not be able to approach her directly.

"I noticed that you left early from the last fundraiser. Weren't you enjoying yourself? The food, beverages, and music seemed lovely to me. The fund-raiser was a big success. Was there a personal reason that you would like to share?"

"I noticed you were dancing all the time."

"Yes, I was with the lady with the gaudiest jewelry."

"Is there any reason for your doing that that you would like to share?"

Roy laughed. "I like sparkle. My condo sparkles and I like sparkles on ladies—on their shoes, neck, or wrists."

"Well, I guess we'll never get to dance." She immediately regretted saying this last comment knowing that he would pick it up and challenge her as he sought to move forward. After another second, she thought that might be fun. It had been a long time since she had been with a man.

"I think *never* is a terrible word and should be banned from public usage. It should only be used for historical facts as in 'The Native Americans were never able to repurchase Manhattan Island.'"

"I'll try to never use never again."

"Good. Now, would you like a drink or is that going to be something you never do with me?"

Sonia found herself in bed after two drinks. His lovemaking had a steely quality. It was satisfying, but she knew this man did not have a tender side.

"This is a lovely way to spend an afternoon." He paused draw a breath and said softly. "I'd like to see you again."

Sonia was taken aback. "Let me think about that." She knew that this would just be a liaison based on sex. She was not opposed to that, but there was also something about him that was going to be impenetrable. "I don't have any diamonds."

"Well, that's something that can be fixed. Keep the $500 and buy yourself something."

That suggestion convinced her. She would have nothing to do with this man but would not tell him now.

"That's generous and thoughtful. I prefer you keep it and let's see where things go with us. As I said, I want to think about it."

They had been lying in bed and started to dress when Sonia had the impulse to ask how well he knew Detective Zuma. She had noticed they had been talking at the fundraiser.

"He's on my case. Thinks I killed Edna. Doesn't like me. Do you know him?"

"Yes, he was on my case a couple of years ago. He thinks I murdered my husband."

"I guess we both hope that our tormentor will take the job in Boston."

"I think I know him pretty well. I don't think he will leave until he genuinely feels we are innocent. He's the kind of guy who would be willing to come up to you or me and apologize. Until that happens, I know he will be searching for clues and be on the lookout. He's a hunter, you know. Going over and over the trails and suspects."

Guy felt a sudden admiration for the woman he had just had sex with. This was an unusual feeling for him. He wondered. His interest in art was not something he ever pursued with the artists who had created it. That she was an artist in wood appealed and even excited him. He thought he would like to pursue her even if she had no sparkling, glittering diamonds.

"Maybe we can come up with some leads that will convince him he's on the wrong trail."

"I like that idea."

"What did you have in mind?"

"Hear me out. But first I would very much like to visit your work."

Sonia sensed something different in his request.

She did not understand why he had changed the steely self, but he was expressing a need. The male hunter had let his guard down. The female hunter sensed she would be circling her prey.

"I think that could be arranged, and I would like that. But what did you have in mind for getting Zuma off our cases?"

"Well, he thinks you or I were involved with Edna's murder. There was a theft. Suppose I figured out a way to have the painting that was stolen appear in another person's home or work? Or I could have the painting, since I already own one, sent to the precinct with a note of some sort."

"It would have to be a pretty good note and from a person that was so off the radar that he might feel that he had missed a clue."

"I was hoping over a dinner we could figure out the note and who else to blame. I have a brother and a child who might be good suspects."

Sonia saw the steely coldness again. That he had it for others but at this point not with her made her more confident about her likely conquest.

CHAPTER 60

A Handsome Couple

Carl was on time and looked very presentable.

"We are two very normal straights, Carl. I don't think we will scare anyone, and I don't think we look like cops."

"I haven't been dressed up like this for a very long time. Take a picture, Mary, so I can send it to my brother. I need to show him I can make it as a regular. I think he'll have trouble believing it."

"It's only a first day. We may not be able to do this on consecutive days. It depends on how successful we are. If we run out of stuff, I will have to go back tomorrow to score some more, unless you want to do that."

"It will take me some time to figure out another connection. I could do that tomorrow while you are picking up some more stuff."

"Let's not jump the gun and see how well we do today. I think we should start in the valley. North Hills, Pasadena, and Van Nuys should be good. I know those places. I slept there."

The two of them worked smoothly together. None of the straights balked when they approached. One homeless person was testy but was quieted down when another one assured him, "She was one of us. She's cool." They were so successful with selling that they never got to Van Nuys.

"I guess we have to spend tomorrow building up our supplies. How would you like to handle the money? We can keep a record and divvy it up at the end of a week or wait until we reach $1000 before we divvy it up. Or we can just split it down the middle as we go."

Carl was not used to waiting or trusting "Down the middle every time we do a day is fine. How much do we have today?"

"Let me pull over and we can count it."

"$780 bucks. I never came close to that on the bluffs. I guess if you wear a suit you just make more money."

"You're probably right, Carl. And the most expensive suits make the most money."

She didn't want to ask Carl what he was going to do with the money, but she was going to open up a savings and a checking account right away. She would need that to get an apartment and for a job application. She was grateful that this time selling was going to be limited. Carl was nice now but could prove to be unreliable.

They were out again on Wednesday and Friday.

They had collected $2,300.00. At this pace, she believed she could stop the work in two months. Mary wanted to work on Saturday, but Carl balked, and they agreed to do Sunday.

She thought of going out on her own on Saturday. How could she justify selling stuff and pocketing the money? Maybe she would split it even though he was not working with her. She was sure that would not work, as she believed no matter how honest she was that Carl would not believe her. She also had to figure out how to pay back Zuma. She couldn't just show up with the full $297.00. And if she told him she had found a job, he would check on her to make sure. She felt that Zuma would just have to wait. She would let him know she hadn't found work as yet but had filled out applications, had nice clothes, but so far, no bites.

The security at the desk stared with disbelief. "I didn't know Mr. Roy had a brother. I'm sure he'll be happy to see you. I trust your ID, but I can't just let you go up. I'm under strict orders. We've recently had a murder in the building. It was pretty gruesome. Sorry, I will have to announce you."

Carl knew about Edna's demise but thought better of saying anything personal.

"Yes, I read about that in the papers."

"My god, brother, you really look good in your clothes. I always hoped that being a hobo would just be a temporary thing. Do you think you want a regular job?"

"Woah, Guy, don't push it."

"Okay, so did you drop in just to show off your new clothes or is there something you want from me or that I can do for you?"

"Yes, there is. I'm going to say it straight. I want you to get rid of someone."

Guy's first thought was that Carl must be high. He looked at him and saw he was deadly serious and not glassy eyed.

"Carl, I'm sorry. I'm not in that kind of business. Are you in some trouble or danger with this person?"

"Not at this point. I was just thinking about the future."

"Do you want to tell me what this involves? I could at least start to think about it. Maybe there are other solutions."

"I think I'll wait to talk with you. Things may change. Thanks for your offer to listen."

Carl was polite to the security guard as he left but was furious at his brother. Guy always thought of himself first. Maybe it wasn't such a good idea in the first place to have him do anything. If he did, he would always have it over him that a request was made. He realized that he would have to get rid of Mary on his own. He also recalled that Guy already had something on him about the Truro murder. Maybe he would be able to figure out a way to get rid of both of them. If he were to wear a suit, he had to be concerned with someone taking him down. As a hobo, he never had far to fall. Tomorrow was Sunday and that was always a good day for selling. He couldn't think of anything better than wearing a suit in outdoors sunny California, not scaring people away, and making money.

CHAPTER 61

America Is a Strange Place

"Mr. and Mrs. Schnable, Pat and I want to thank you for coming in. We want to hear about what you have found from teaching in the school."

He spoke first. "Thank you for letting us do this. It has helped us feel closer to Hope and to understand why she loved these children so much. They are so bright and full of ideas."

"Yes, Detective Zuma. We do love working there and the extra money also helps. It looks like we will be able to take the trip back to Germany with a number of them."

"Have you noticed any signs of drug usage or some kids flashing money?"

"Many of them seem tried but I think that's because of the pressure. You Americans really push children. You rush them toward adulthood. Childhood is a special time. Unlike any other, it should be filled with success and joy and fun. Our Hope understood that and that is why she was such a good teacher. The older ones like to strut, especially the boys, but they don't use money to show off. It's usually about who's stronger or faster."

"Mr. Tapper are you comfortable with the Schnables leading a group from your school?"

Yes, Detective Zuma. They have done an excellent job here. The kids all love them. And we should be able to get a parent or two to go with them to ensure that there is ongoing supervision. They will have to fill out a number of forms and have to do interviews as immigrants responsible for American children."

"We would like to take younger children rather than the older ones. The older ones are less curious and would see it as an opportunity to run wild. I hope, Mr. Tapper, that you can understand that."

"I do and I'll place an ad that specifies an age range that you feel comfortable with."

"Mr. and Mrs. Schnable. Thank you again for your efforts to help us reduce drug usage in the school. If anything unusual comes up, you can always get hold of Pat or me. I need to check with my superiors about speaking favorably about the two of you in a court hearing. I don't believe that there should be a problem with your prior violations. There might be a fine. We should start this process now to make you ready for your return to Germany."

"Thank you to all of you. America is a strange place. You have so many wonderful people who are generous and kind in a country that is punitive and neglects the less fortunate."

Zuma, Pat, and Tapper smiled as the Schnables exited.

"Pat, I think if we get the same report from Jensen. We can take him out of his role. Mr. Tapper, you asked us to wait until the fundraiser was over so you could leave your school in good financial shape. You have done that. I think it is time to book you for knowledge of drug use in your school and failure to report drug usage in your school. Your board should also know about the free tuition you provided to a parent."

"Detective, the spring semester is almost over. If I can be allowed to finish my term, the publicity about me will be less damaging to the school's efforts to recruit potential teachers and new applicants for the following year. I will not challenge the guilty charges in court and hope that my efforts here will be looked upon favorably by you and by the court."

"I can wait, Mr. Tapper. I will be appearing on June first. Would you please provide me with your passport?"

"Of course. And thank you."

"Okay, Pat, I think we can rule out the Schnables and Tapper as suspects for any of the murders. I also think that Jack can be ruled out. Who does that leave us?"

"Boss, it's Roy, his brother, and the furniture maker."

"I get kind of queasy when all the leads seem to point so clearly to one person."

"Boss, you always told me to follow the leads but not to ignore my instincts."

"And what do your instincts tell you, Pat?"

"That something or someone is missing. If it isn't Roy, I would put my money on the woman you thought was guilty in the murder of her husband. If you do it once, a second is easier. The brother is a great big puzzle. He's educated but a hobo. He's a hobo with an apartment supported by a brother. Just puzzles the hell out of me."

CHAPTER 62

Fresh Starts, Old Ways

Mary Follette had saved enough money for first and last month's deposit in Van Nuys. She could have afforded Brentwood but thought that would make Zuma suspicious. Her efforts to secure a position were also successful. The shutdown by Trump opened up a lot of positions in security at the airport. As she was strong, she was not worried about what kind of position they would be giving her. Even if she had to lift baggage all day long for inspection, she knew that would be fine. She felt that Zuma would feel good that he had helped her with the car and that she had paid back his loan to her. The information she had provided him with the regular and straight users on the bluffs accompanied by pictures would be helpful to Zuma. Her only concern was Carl. She had not had any difficulty with him but believed that it was because of the small amount of marijuana that she gave him every day. She knew it calmed him. She was worried about what he might do when she no longer wanted to deal. She could seduce him in order to make him feel more loyal but only saw that as a short-term solution to the problem of his loyalty. The more she thought about it the closer she came to the idea that Carl had to go.

Carl was distraught. "That son of a bitch Zuma is back on my case. He hauled me into the precinct and showed me the hobo painting. He said the person who murdered Roy's wife stole it from her. He said there was a note indicating that I had murdered her. The signer said they were afraid to give their name because of my mental illness. Mary, you and my brother are the only ones who think I have a mental illness. It must have been my friggin' brother who did this. You wouldn't want to break up our team, would you?"

"No, Carl, I wouldn't do anything like that. But listen. Have they found a weapon? No, they haven't. Do they have any motive for you? No! What could you possibly gain from her death? It's not like there's an insurance policy. And they actually have no evidence of your stealing the painting. There is no photo, no digital security evidence. I think Zuma is just blowing smoke. And since he is smart, he must have had another motive for calling you in."

"Damn, you're smart. Do I have a lawsuit against him for false charges?"

"No, I'm sure you don't. But what might he have had in mind by this effort to accuse you knowing that he had no case? I think it must have something to do with your brother."

"What something is that?"

"Well, Carl, most people know you have a temper and what you might do if you were to get mad at your brother. Do you have knowledge of things he did that if you were to go to the cops would get him in trouble with the law?"

"Of course, I do."

"Well, maybe Zuma is hoping you will send a note that has better evidence than the one he received."

"I could do that, but the problem is, Mary, that most of the things that I know my brother did also involve me."

"If you're thinking about letting Zuma know that your brother was a supplier that would involve you, Zuma already knows that you have dealt drugs. He must be hoping for something bigger."

"The bigger thing, Mary, also involves me."

"Okay, I guess the best strategy is to not write a note or to do anything. You keep your secrets and business to yourself."

Mary knew that the bigger thing must be a murder. She did not want to pry and find out whom. If Carl confessed to her, she knew she would be less safe with him than she already felt. A plan began to formulate on how Carl could go. But first she had to clear things up with Zuma. She needed to give him back his money, and the information she had gathered about the bluffs as well as an update on her life.

"Detective Zuma, I'm glad you could see me. I have all the money that you laid out for me. It's a money order. I also want to let you know that I am no longer living out of my car. I took a one-bedroom unfurnished place in the valley. I now live in Van Nuys. I had no trouble sleeping with the place being unfurnished. It was much better than my car. I have been slowly furnishing the place. I also lucked out with a job. TSA lost a lot of people who couldn't survive without a weekly paycheck. I was hired and have been working for over a month. I'm registered in an evening class for court stenography so our paths may never cross again. Detective, I hope those pictures I took of the regular straight buyers on the bluffs will prove successful."

"Happy that I could help you land on your feet, Mary. You were a good investment. Goodbye to you and you have my best wishes."

Mary left. She knew that Zuma would be checking on her work site and her new residence. She had covered all her bases. Now she could focus on Carl.

"Pat, let's use these photos to identify those straight folks on the bluffs. Don't lock them up. I don't want any wholesale arrests. Pick one of our younger men or women who you think is sharp. Have them use the pics to identify these folks. We don't want any heavy threats. Just have our guy warn them if they ever appear to be buying, we will use the pics as evidence. Make copies of the pics and have the person hand it to the buyer. This will remind them that we know who they are."

"Okay, boss, I'm on it."

CHAPTER 63

Pillow Talk, without Pillows

Their lovemaking had taken on a distinctive pattern. Guy was stiff and hard and brittle in their first effort. It was not perfunctory, but it was his assertion of dominance and power. If they were to have another round, he was vulnerable. Sonia always pressed for this as she felt that it was important to and for her to have him get to a sense of need for her. His way of expressing his need for her was through helping her—helping her advertise more, helping her get a bigger studio, and helping her with purchasing newer and better tools. She knew that allowed him to feel and be in control. She turned these offers down, hoping to frustrate him so that he would search for other ways, emotional ways, that he could express his need for her and his feelings of admiration. He admired silently when he sat and watched her work on wood. He admired with words after their lovemaking about her intelligence, beauty, and focus. He began to realize that his love of art had avoided thinking about the artist. Now that he was close to one, it brought him closer to the art that he had also admired but had maintained a distance from.

Guy Roy had never felt a desire to merge with someone. For him, it was always power and control over the women he was wooing and bedding and marrying. This was new. He was warmed by the feeling but wary. He was unsure about what was going to happen to them. He was always able to control the future of all the relationships he had. He had done that with his wives, his brother, and his children.

Now because Sonia did not want to appear in public with him, he was unable to take her to the best restaurants or go to museums. She had rejected all his offers of financial help and for a weekend getaway, citing her desire to not leave Lucy. He was restricted to being with her in her apartment. She did not want to have their trysts in his building because the security would eventually get to know her. She was clearly keeping their relationship under wraps. When he would arrive at her building, he would ring the buzzer, look down to see if it was him and buzz him in. Very few people saw him. That's the way she wanted it.

"So, you sent the painting with a note. Did anything happen that made you feel that Zuma was doing anything?"

"No. I'm sure they want to check it for fingerprints and anything else that would lead them to the sender but so far nothing has happened. I did get an urgent call from my brother this morning but since I was going to be with you, I decided not to respond.

"Sonia, when we met early on, we both said that Zuma was on our case, me for murdering my wife and you for murdering your husband. Would you ever trust me to tell me if you did it?"

Sonia laughed. "You are a silly man, Guy. If you knew something like that you would be a potential witness against me. Why would I do that?"

"And If I told you something about me that could send me off to prison, you could be a potential witness against me. I would be willing to do that. And I have an idea how we can protect each other even if we know about these possible illegal and murderous affairs."

Sonia knew what he was going to say but went along with it, knowing that this would be a further step in his vulnerability and her control.

"And your idea is…?"

"If we were to marry, we could not—"

"Now you are really being silly."

Sonia now knew he was totally in her control. She decided to make objections that had nothing to do with her deep feeling that she would never want to be married to this man.

"Guy, I have a daughter. You have not met her. Your relationship with her would be critical. She would need to like you and be comfortable with you. We are not even a public item. There are all the logistics of any merger on our part. Shall you move in here? Or should we relocate at your place? I need to have a studio. Would your building allow for that? After all, I am running a business and I do make noise when I'm sawing, sanding, and drilling."

Guy was not disheartened. That she had brought up these issues made him feel that she was at least open to the idea of dealing with them. He was pleased about that. He could successfully address each of the matters she raised. He knew that the biggest challenge that she mentioned was her daughter. He would have to learn how to be with a weak and vulnerable child. He knew that was not what he wanted in either of his marriages. The idea of having a normal life with a normal family was something new to him. Its newness appealed to him as he began thinking about what it could mean to have a family that he looked forward to coming home to.

CHAPTER 64

Brotherly Love

Guy had prepared for his brother. He expected fury and he was getting it.

"There's only one other person who knows about my mental illness and she would never tell anyone so it must have been you who sent that goddamn note to Zuma. You son of a bitch. You're trying to frame me for a murder, and you know I didn't do it."

Guy had no trouble lying. He had grown out of practicing since he was with Sonia, but he easily slipped into his old way.

"I have no idea what you're talking about. I've had nothing to do with Zuma. I have no desire to be in any kind of contact with him. And I don't know what note you are talking about. I have no reason to get you in trouble with the law. I'm doing everything I can to keep you out of jail. You are my brother. If you go to jail, you might use information you have about me to get a better sentence and that would only hurt me."

"I don't trust you, Guy. You know me well that I will spill the beans on you. So, help me God, I will."

"And that is exactly why I would never want to see you threatened with a jail sentence. I like it that you are not selling drugs anymore and that you wear clothes that don't smell or are so shabby that people pity you. I'm comforted that you have an apartment that can keep you off the streets and warm at night. All those things matter to me. I want you to be able to continue living as you do now and not go back to the way you were."

"What about the painting that Zuma received? Was that the one I got for you?"

"Carl, I just told you I had nothing to do with Zuma. Look in the other room, I still have the painting."

Carl left and looked carefully at his likeness. He realized that his brother was lying but decided that he would not say anything about it. He would have to come up with a plan to get rid of Guy for what he had done. His brother was willing to send him off to prison. This was too much. The thought that he would lose income and not afford the apartment along with Mary's refusal to continue working with him did not faze him. Life on the bluffs had never been awful or even bad. He would figure it all out without any help from his lying, son-of-a-bitch brother.

"Okay, Guy, I see you are telling the truth. I apologize. Do you think you could advance me a couple of hundred towards next month's rent?"

"Sure, bro, I'm in your corner and will always be there."

Carl left thinking that the corner would soon be less crowded without a brother."

CHAPTER 65

Partners Reunited

"Mary, he lied to me. He thought I would fall for his brotherly love statements, but I figured out that he was lying."

"He told me that he had nothing to do with any painting that Zuma had received and invited me to see that he still had his. When I went in the other room, I saw that the number on the painting was different from the one I had given him. I nearly busted out screaming but held it in and left. But not before I got an advance on the rent."

"What do you think you're going to do?"

"I don't know. I want to, no I need to, get rid of him but haven't figured out a way. Do you think you can help me?"

Mary had to think. She was planning to off Carl. Carl wanted to off Guy. Should she wait till he did it? Should she help him? Would it be better for her if Carl were out of the way? She was sure that Zuma would be sure that Guy had done it. How would this affect her? Would Zuma be less involved than ever with her situation? She liked that idea. The death of two brothers from Santa Monica would make for big headlines and lots of pressure on Zuma. But she also knew that it would be much better for her if Carl was out of the way and that Zuma would pursue Guy. She formulated her plan.

"Carl, let's go back in business for one more month. I would like to have a bit more cash for a rainy day. Would you be willing to do that?"

"Sure, Mary, I love working with you."

"Okay, I'll get enough drugs to sell for the next couple of weeks." She thought it would take her a bit less than two weeks to get rid of her partner. "I can get a bunch of stuff tomorrow and we can start the day after."

"Great, Mary, can we celebrate?"

She felt she could drop her guard. "Sure, lets meet for dinner. I'll pick you up tomorrow night after I have gotten all our supplies. We can plan out the next few days of work. Do you have a place you'd like to eat? I'll treat."

"I like the Shangri-La."

"Good, Carl, I'll make the reservation for seven. We need to be dressed so we won't be conspicuous in that restaurant."

Carl realized that she had never been so friendly. He was pleased to see this shift in her attitude. He liked that she was forward about the invitation as well as her willingness to pick up the tab. His hope for something more than a business arrangement was kindled. He planned to pick up a large bouquet of flowers for her. That was something he had never done before. He was imitating the straights whom he had seen do that kind of thing.

CHAPTER 66

Ending an Affair

As their relationship continued into the spring, Sonia was feeling less resolve than she felt at the beginning of their affair. She knew from her first marriage and from conversations with girlfriends that husbands don't change. Men often make promises they will act differently in the future but changes that are made rarely endure. She was surprised that he had not been fazed by the fact that she was Jewish and had a last name that identified her as such.

She had seen parts of Guy that she was sure he had never exposed to anyone before, even perhaps to himself. Change would have to be initiated by Guy. She was both hopeful that he might be able to do that but realistic that it was pretty unlikely. If Lucy were going to be away in Germany with her schoolmates, she would be alone. If she ended it before then, she would have a summer without him. She was not looking forward to being alone. She had seen his efforts to change. He talked less about facts, his successes, and his business and more about his feelings. He continued to be interested in her work and asked her questions about the wood she was using and designs she was developing.

He rarely told her what to do but made suggestions along the lines "Have you thought about this other way of finishing the sitting chair" or "There's a brand-new restaurant in Pasadena and if you are up for going out please let me know." He no longer pushed to see Lucy or to go out. She believed he was getting better with developing patience. But she still kept Lucy away from him and still refused to be seen in public. If Lucy was going to be away for the summer, she knew he would be more ardent, and she would have difficulty seeing him less often. Ending the relationship would be difficult, and she did not want to end it the way she had done with her first husband. She was hoping that he would find a reason to not continue. She began thinking of reasons he might want to end it or make it difficult for him to continue with the same intensity. Money and power seemed less important to him now. He had three children. Could they become reasons for him to modify his attachment to her? She wondered if his getting to see and love Lucy would open him up to his daughter and two sons. She was worried about Lucy becoming too attached. Maybe she could time it so that Lucy would leave for Germany before he became deeply involved and connected to her. She was not in love with her idea but saw no other way of getting rid of him. Except for murder. Maybe some other idea would come to her. There was no rush.

CHAPTER 67

Simple Plans

Guy had given up on his brother. He was no longer deeply ashamed about his twin being a hobo or upset about his monthly stipend or his continued use of drugs. He knew he was never going to have any relationship other than that which occurred when Carl needed money. He was a thorn in the side. Being pricked once a month had taken a toll. His last outburst accusing him of trying to frame him was more than a pinprick. It was a smash to his head. He began devising a plan to get rid of him. It seemed simple. Dress up like Carl the hobo. Go to the palisades where Carl hung out and kill some old defenseless woman. He would make sure that he would be seen only by a straight. He knew that other hobos would see through his disguise as well as his demeanor. He needed soiled or dirty and torn clothes and something to smudge his face. It would have to be done towards dusk when the light was fading. It seemed simple. Much simpler than the last murder.

Mary Follette had also devised a simple plan that took her a little longer to implement. After their successful days of selling in the Valley, she had invited Carl for walks on the beach. He began counting on the time she would spend with him and began hoping that she had a change of heart.

They would not talk much. He was content with handholding. He found that it was better if she took the lead. While sitting on the beach, she would give him some marijuana laced with opiates. They watched the sunset every evening. She increased the dosage every day. He did not notice the slight differences in taste or smell while smoking. He would feel romantic and warm. He felt quite warm as he took his last breath. She got up quietly while his body slumped over. She was unsure if the tide would come in far enough to take his body out. She realized it didn't matter. The body would be discovered either on the beach or because it had been washed ashore somewhere. She had made sure to put his ID in the back pocket of his pants that had a button.

She walked slowly back from the shore and to her car. She felt that she would be safe, and she decided to dine at the Shangri-La as a way of thanking Carl for how he had helped her.

"Boss, this is almost impossible to believe. We got a call from the ME this morning. Guy Roy's brother's body was found on the beach near the pier. The fishes had not gotten to him, since the body was in the water for just one night. He was easy to identify since he had an ID in his pants."

"It's an obvious ploy. Someone else must have done this to make us think that Roy did. If Roy did, I'm sure he has a well-established alibi. I think we need to think who else might want Mr. Hobo out of the picture. How many bodies do we have now, Pat?"

"It's up to four, boss. More bodies mean less suspects, don't you think?"

"Unless we are completely missing the boat on possible suspects."

"Let's go back and figure out any if there are any, no matter how seemingly unrelated to these murders. I mean unrelated, like the Schnables or Hope's boyfriend. We'll do our likely and unlikely lists and start again."

"Okay, boss, I'll have the list by this afternoon."

Zuma decided that it would be better to deliver the news in person about Carl's murder. He also felt he needed to tell Claudia about the man she had made famous.

"Joe, that is sad. I had hoped that he would have been able to get to a better place in his life. I guess, sometimes, there is too much baggage you carry or just too many barriers."

"Claudia, he had baggage and barriers. It's a minor miracle that you preserved an image of him that many will see. He will be known or seen by many more now that he has gone than when he was alive."

"Joe, that would not make any difference to him now."

"You're right, darling. No matter how many people show up at a funeral, it makes no difference to the deceased."

"If his brother has anything to do with it, and I think he will, Carl's body will be cremated."

"Joe, can we go out to dinner tonight? I would like to have a quiet dinner. We can go to Shangri-La. But give me an hour or so. I want to see if I can do something more with Carl. I'd like to do another quick sketch that I will use later as a painting."

"Sure. I can go listen to Newman's 'I Think It's Gonna Rain Today' while I wait for you. It certainly has poured. By the way, I have discovered a tune that I have fallen in love with. It's from that silly movie, *The Umbrellas of Cherbourg*. They made the movie to be like an opera. No dialogue. Everybody sings to each other. But there is this song, which I keep singing to myself. I'm trying to learn the words in French and in English."

"What is it? I don't think I know the movie."

"The English title is 'I Will Wait for You,' and the first line is 'If it takes forever, I will wait for you.'"

Claudia smiled and nodded her head as if to say, "What a romantic."

"It won't take me forever, Joe. Just an hour or so."

"I'll play it over dinner, I can get it on my cell. Michel Legrand sings it with his wife."

Claudia left the room to change, nodding her head from side to side singing the words and lyrics to "You Are the Wind beneath My Wings." As she stepped into the shower, she thought it was wonderful that she was never bored by Joe's romantic ways.

CHAPTER 68

Solid Alibis

Pat and Joe sat silently for a long time looking at the names. They were perplexed and felt stumped. The medical examiner had done an autopsy and found opiates in Carl's body and they thought of the Schnables. But they could not think of how they or Sonia could have or would have wanted to get rid of Carl. All of them could provide evidence that they were busy with other things on the evening Carl was murdered. Everything pointed to Guy. But he also had an alibi for the evening. He and his son had been out together from about 4:30 on. Roy had refused to say where they had been but was willing to take a lie detector test and indicate that if it came to a court trial that his testimony and that of his son and another person would vindicate him.

"That was only one son. There is another. Seems very unlikely but we need to check it out."

"Boss, who could this other person be who would Guy be visiting. He's not exactly Mr. Friendly."

"I don't know, Pat. We need to put another tail on him. Let's find out if the visits are a regular thing. We can interview all the people that he has become chummy with. This would be a big change or shift for him. Maybe if we can figure out why this is happening, it could lead us to another person. Maybe Guy got someone to do the deed."

CHAPTER 69

Diagnostic Reconsideration

"Your hunch to tail Guy paid off. He has been visiting your old suspect three times a week.

"Must be a woman, right, Pat? But I can't imagine any woman who is an old suspect. Oh my god, wait a minute. Are you going to tell me that Guy Roy and the furniture lady murder suspect are seeing each other?"

"Yes, boss. It will probably shock you just as much if I tell you he shows up with flowers every time he visits."

"That is a hard one to believe. Good that we now know whom. I wonder why? If Milgram were right, he would never be interested in anyone else but himself."

"Boss, you always told me how powerful love can be."

Yes, I did, Pat. But Milgram said that it would be highly unlikely for Roy to feel kindness, empathy, or affection for anyone. Those are feelings that accompany a sense of love."

"Maybe you should give Milgram a call."

"Dr. Milgram, the sociopath has been visiting a woman three times a week. He shows up with flowers and when he leaves later, he is smiling. Can this be possible?"

"Detective Zuma, anything is possible, but I have my doubts. He might be faking it in order to obtain something he wants but can't get directly with force. Do you think you can bring him in so I can observe him again? I have been wrong before. Some people, very few, can change.

I'm happy to be of help and if I was wrong, I will be happy to see improvement."

Zuma felt lots of respect for Milgram. He was willing to admit that he had been mistaken. He was not sure that at this time he would call Roy in for another observation.

CHAPTER 70

Hearts and Flowers

Sonia was shocked to see Zuma and his assistant at the front door.

"Detective, I've said this to you before. I don't know how many times I have to repeat it to you. I know nothing more about my husband's disappearance."

"This is about something else Mrs. Tabachnick. I'm hoping you will cooperate and answer some questions or give us some information."

"I will not say yes to that unless I know the questions you want answered or the information you would like."

She was tough as ever.

"We know that Mr. Guy Roy has been visiting you at least three nights a week for the last two weeks. It may have been longer, but we definitely know that. Could you tell us if you and he are romantically involved?"

"That, Detective Zuma, is none of your business."

"Are you involved in any business plans or financial arrangements?"

"I could repeat the same answer, but I would be boring."

"We notice that when Mr. Roy visits that your daughter is never here. Do you have a reason for keeping the two of them apart?"

"Again, not your business."

"Do you plan to ever meet his children?"

"Detective, this is getting tiresome. If you were to ask me about my work, my plans for designing new furniture, I would be happy to respond with complete candor. My personal, social, and professional life is off base to you. I'm not a suspect, so unless you have questions about my furniture, I'm going to ask you to leave."

"Boss, she was as helpful as she always has been. Zero. Nada."

"Yes, Pat, but we have planted something for her to think and maybe worry about. She may be worried that Roy is a suspect, and this may make her more hesitant to be with him. If she makes any changes, it may affect him. Remember, he is rigid. Anything we can do to ruffle him might help us. Let's keep a tail on her and see if 'Mr. Heart and Flowers' continues to show."

The toothpick had come out and Zuma was humming. Pat knew it was not "Papa Was a Rolling Stone."

CHAPTER 71

The Funeral

The service for Carl Roy was held at the Santa Monica Catholic Church. Guy Roy wanted as much recognition and good PR as he could get for the funeral of his brother. It did not bother him that very few people would show up or that the church was so much larger than the small gathering for Carl. He made sure that the newspaper clipping reported that he had made all the arrangements and would mention that the church was famous for having been the setting for one of the most famous of all Bing Crosby's hits, "Going My Way". He was going to get good press by asking that all donations should be sent to him, Guy Roy, in order to establish what Carl loved the most, "benches" on the bluffs. He insisted that his sons show up for their uncle, and it was the first time that he had seen his daughter. He admired her clothes and looks. She was a beauty. A few of Carl's hobo friends stayed in the rear away from the family who sat in the first row. A few people from his condo apartment showed up and he also noticed that there was a well-dressed woman who sat alone, not too far from the hobos and a greater distance from his family. All in all, there was not a baker's dozen people who had come to the service and only six or seven knew Carl. The service was impersonal and short. That is what Guy had wanted. He had asked Sonia to show up, but she had turned him down. Even when he begged her, she had refused. As the priest spoke, Guy's mind wandered as he gazed out at his progeny. The introductions with them had been awkward but they seemed comfortable to be there. There would be no graveside ceremony because of the planned cremation so he had hoped that his three children would come to his condo or perhaps he would be able to take them for lunch. After exiting the church, he made sure to corner them asking them to dine. Edwin put his arm around his sister, "Give us a moment, Guy, we need to discuss it." This put him off but what he had learned from Sonia paid off.

"Sure, whatever you need to do will be fine with me. I would like it, however, and it would mean a lot to me if we could all be together. You could pick the kind of food you want."

When the children moved away to talk, the woman whom he did not recognize approached.

"You don't know me, Mr. Roy, but I knew your brother pretty well. I used to be in the same life that he was in. Fortunately, I have been able to put my life together. I liked Carl a lot. He was a kind man. The other vagrants and I felt very comfortable with him. They knew he would never steal stuff and would not hurt them. He looked out for me when some of them were threatening. He was a good man, and I'm sorry for your loss. Are those children nephews and a niece of Carl's?"

"Yes, they are. It's unfortunate they did not know their uncle well. He was not exactly available."

Guy felt eerie describing his brother in that way. He recognized that the words "not available" applied to him even more strongly. Mary walked away before he could ask her name.

Zuma and Pat had been sitting in the church for the entire service. Mary Follette had nodded to Zuma on her way out and knew that she would have to speak with him before she left.

"Hi, Detective Zuma. Nice to see you even under these circumstances. I hope you received my money order, and I want to thank you again for having been helpful to me at a time I was in dire straits.

"You are quite welcome. Now that we are meeting, could you give me the address where you live and the number where you work?"

"Sure. Let me write them down. Are you planning to ask me to do more spying? I don't think I would be willing to do that."

"No, I just need it for our files."

The three children approached. "Guy, we want to go to lunch." Guy gulped and held his breath. "And we would like to eat Thai food." He still had not heard what he was hoping to hear. It came shortly after their request. "Can we all go in one car?"

CHAPTER 72

Trying for Togetherness

Sonia heard an excitement in Guy's voice that she had never heard before. "I must see you. Please. I had all my kids to lunch, and I need to talk with you."

"Sure, give me an hour. I just finished up staining a piece and I need to wash up. If you're hungry, you need to pick up something. My cupboard is bare."

He picked up her favorite piazza, a bottle of chianti, cupcakes, and a large bouquet of sunflowers which he knew were here favorite.

"It was pretty embarrassing, Sonia. They asked me all kind of questions about Carl. What he liked to eat, his favorite music, any hobbies, why he hadn't married. Why did he like living as a hobo. Even though I felt stupid not knowing very much about him, it just felt good to be asked the questions. I did tell them that he had some mental problems that made it difficult for him to have relationships, have girlfriends, or a regular job. I also told them I supported him. My daughter is beautiful. She is, I don't know what the right word is, a bit slow. Maybe autistic. But polite and sweet."

Sonia was pleased for Guy and that this was what she had hoped for. This could turn out to be the attachment that would diminish his need for her making it easier for her to break it off.

"How did the four of you leave it?"

"Well, that was the strangest part. They said good-bye as one "We have to go now." They must have planned it. I said that I would

188

like to take them out again. Edward said he would have to discuss it. They are a tight bunch. I didn't know what to make of it. I don't know if they will call."

"Give them some time, Guy. After a week or so, give them a ring. Work through the ringleader, not your bodyguard."

That last word was a hammer to his head. He would have to change the way he employed and approached his son.

"I'm going to need your help on how to change my relationship with Edwin."

"I can help you with that. Let's finish the wine and go to bed. I've had a long day and it seems that you have had a long and challenging day also."

In her bedroom, after lovemaking, Guy asked, "Do you think I could have Lucy and my kids meet? I think she would really like my Sarah."

"Patience, dear, patience."

CHAPTER 73

A Rubik's Cube

"Boss, I called that phone number and went to the address that the Follette woman gave you. She's not at that address and does not work at the job. I don't think it was an accident that she gave out phony information."

"I did think it was pretty quick that she got back on her feet. She would have had to come up with two months' rent. That's a lot for someone who had been living in a car. But, Pat, she is nimble and quick. Maybe she really was able to earn all that money."

"Is there some way we can track her down?"

"She paid for the towing with a money order so there is no checking account we could follow up on. I think we will have to go back to the bluffs to see if anyone has an idea of where she might be and what she might be doing."

"We can do that pretty easily, boss, but do you realize how crazy this is? We have five murder victims and five suspects. We have major suspects in Guy, and now possibly Mary and Sonia. Minor possibilities are Guy's children, Tapper, Jack, and the Schnables. How could they possibly be connected?"

"Let's remove the Schnables and Jack. That leaves us with five victims and five suspects.

Guy knew three of the vics. Sonia knew two, and we know that Mary knew at least one. Are the suspects connected? Guy and Sonia now know each other, though they may not have known one another in the past. Mary seems to be without connection to the others."

"It's a Rubik's cube, boss."

"I know, Pat. We just have to keep trying to move it around and around."

"Sure, but where do we start?"

"We try and find Mary. Let's go to all the banks in the LA area and ask them to do a search for Mary Follette and all folks who have opened new accounts in the past few months. You can get an order from the court to do that. Let's get her picture. We can get it from the towing service. I know they either took one of her or they have a copy of her registration. You can bring it down to the bluffs and ask around to see if she has been seen coming around. If someone recognizes her, ask if they noticed anything different about her. We can also use her car registration to see if the DMV has a new address for her. She is supposed to provide one when she fills out a new registration application. Let's see if that helps. I think between all of these, we should be able to find out where our homeless lady is now living. I want to hold off on bringing Sonia Tabachnick or Mr. Hearts and Flowers in. Let's try Tapper again. I have some thoughts."

CHAPTER 74

Tres Leches

It had been four consecutive weeks that Guy's children had gone to dinner with him. They had tried different restaurants with different types of food. He was pleased that they seemed to be so eager to explore. They let slip out comments about their past or likes. When he had asked once about their mother, Sarah said that her favorite food was Mexican and that was why she always wanted to eat Mexican food. Her brothers had outvoted her, but they were willing to go on this night. They went to the very happy and friendly Mercado on Fourth Street. He had prepared what he was going to say and spoke when their favorite dessert of tres leches cake arrived.

"I have decided I'd like to make money available to each of you on a monthly basis and for your futures. I can set up an educational fund that will cover your college tuition and go towards living expenses. If you decide you don't want to go to college, you can use the money for whatever training you seek to get. I can also give you each a monthly allowance based on your needs for food, gas, utilities, rent, and some extra spending money for fun. If this is satisfactory, I can have my lawyers draw up contracts for each of you to sign."

"So, I could buy dolls every month?" Sara squealed.

"That is generous, but we do have to talk it over, and we have to all agree to the same thing. We all say yes or we all say no."

Sarah chimed in. "But I don't see why we should say no. No is not good."

"Take your time. It might make for big changes in your lives. Why don't you get back to me? If you give it a green light. maybe, we can sign the papers in my apartment. I want you to know that I'll set it up so that the contract cannot be changed unless both parties agree to it. And when I die, there is enough there for twenty or so years, plus there will be an inheritance which I will divide equally among the three of you. That should carry you into your late fifties. Edward, I have put you in charge of Sarah's monies, and if something should happen to you, your brother can take it over. The educational fund for Sarah could mean any kind of program or tutoring that helps her with her development."

"Sonia, I did it. I told them about a monthly stipend, an educational fund, and an inheritance. They were remarkably cool except for Sarah who was excited because she saw lots of dolls coming her way."

"That's great, Guy." Sonia was impressed. "What you did is so much better than putting money towards having a building named after you."

"I also want to set something up for you and Lucy, but I know that I have to discuss it with you first."

"Yes, you do."

CHAPTER 75

The Hobo Finds a Home

Guy had overordered. There was Mexican, Chinese, Italian, and Thai food and milkshakes and ice cream. He had also bought two big panda dolls. They were coming to sign the contracts they had agreed to over the phone. He rolled out the contracts after he had cleared the table. He hadn't asked Edwin to clean or prepare anything. He had changed the way he related to his son. There were no great smiles or expressions of appreciation forthcoming, but Guy had learned to be patient.

"I have taken myself out of any aspects of controlling this money. We will never have to discuss money again. If you have questions or you need something, just call the lawyer. He will be your lawyer. I have my own. I have appointed you, Edward, as being in charge of Sarah's allowance and future funding. If something happens to you, then Edwin will be in charge."

Sarah was first to speak. "Can I have that picture of Uncle Carl? I know he is not dressed nicely but I see the kindness in his face."

"It is fine with me, Sarah, but I know the way the three of you work, so it seems that the others will have to agree."

The boys each nodded yes.

"Would you like to take it home with you tonight?"

"Yes, but I can't carry it with my pandas."

"Well, what I would like to do, Sarah, is put a really nice frame on it and put it under glass so that it will be with you forever. I'll need a few days to get that done. As soon as it's ready, I'll call you and you can come and pick it up. Would you like to pick out a frame or will you leave that up to me?"

"You pick it out."

Guy said good night and sat quietly gazing out at the lights from the Santa Monica pier and the spinning Ferris wheel. He was spinning with pleasure and a sense of accomplishment.

He had started out with a desire to do everything he could to obtain the painting and protect himself from public scrutiny and possible embarrassment. He had worked hard, even though much of it was illegal to obtain wealth. He was now ending up with giving away what he had spent so much time amassing. The painting had been the cause of grief and a murder. He believed that it would now be in a place where not only the children would enjoy it but anyone else that would be involved in the children's lives could also be helped. He had wanted the picture of Carl for himself and for it not to be seen. The children would probably be proud to show it to anyone they knew and not be embarrassed to say "This was my Uncle Carl. He was a very kind hobo."

His brother was finally able to do something in death that he could not quite do in life—bring happiness to his kin and to others.

CHAPTER 76

Double Pressure

"Boss, we found Follette's address. She's living in the Valley. She changed one number when she handed her address to you. She probably will say it was an accident. It took me some time, but I finally located her, and I have seen her leave early in the morning to work."

"Great, Pat. Visit her and make it seem that the incorrect address was an accident but that your visit was to make sure it was she. Tell her we need to have it for our records."

Zuma could now speak to Tapper about Guy Roy and Mary Follette.

"Mr. Tapper, could you get back to Mr. Roy and ask him to pay you for the tuition that you had granted him? And can you tell him that you are going to tell the police that he failed to report the use of drugs in school?"

"You have me over a barrel, Detective Zuma. I know I am going to be put on trial for my failures. What do I have to gain from this or what does the school have to gain?"

"Your school picks up some money that it did not have. You continue to gain my good will. And the idea that you are going to the police might get you a lot more money from Roy."

Zuma did not believe that Roy would feel threatened by Tapper, but he wanted to keep as much pressure on him as possible.

"I have another request. I would like you to pay a visit to a Ms. Mary Follette."

"I don't know her. What do you want me to do?"

I want you to tell her who you are. Indicate that you overheard her talking to Guy Roy at Carl's service. Also tell her that you asked me for her address. She won't believe any of this but that doesn't matter. You then say to her that Guy was involved in selling drugs and that you had cooperated with him by letting him use the school for selling. You wondered if she would have any interest in doing that. She will say no and how she is now a working woman. On the way out, casually ask her about Carl and her relationship with him."

"Detective, with a question like that, she'll definitely know that my coming out there is a put-up job."

"I'm not worried if she believes it or not. I don't actually expect her to believe your coming to her apartment is something you are doing on your own."

After Tapper agreed and left, Pat asked Joe what he had hoped would happen from Tapper's visit to Follett.

"I just want her to know she still is on our radar. Because she is now employed and living in a regular place doesn't mean that she has changed. We're still waiting to see if she had spent time with Carl prior to his murder. Right?"

CHAPTER 77

A Cracked Skull

"Guy, I can come up and get the painting now."

"I'd like to come down to you so I can see the kids."

"Well, I am alone so why don't I just come up?"

"Boss, we have another believe-it-or-not story. Guy Roy was found in his condo by the cleaning lady this morning at ten. His skull had been cracked open. Our suspects keep dying."

"Pat, it would have to be a pretty damn strong person to crack a skull. We only have three suspects left and all of them are pretty strong. One is Guy's son, whom the Schnables called 'the iceman, two is Guy's lover, 'Ms. Big Chest of Drawers, and three is 'Ms. 'I Lost My House Can You Help Me, Please?'"

"Maybe if we wait a little longer, boss, some of them will also get killed."

"Good one, Pat. I think we have to be ready for a news blitz. I can see the headlines.

Twin Brothers Murdered. Accident or Planned?
No Degrees of Separation between Murdered Brothers."

"Boss, I don't know which of the three would have the most to gain from this murder?"

"Remember, Pat, murder is not always about gain. Sometimes, it's about feelings, like hurt and pain and revenge and self-protection. Let's head over to the fancy condo of Mr. Roy. Call ahead and get the digital recording."

There was no evidence of a forced entry. The item that had been used to crack Roy's skull was a metal statuette that was lying on the floor. The manager had brought up the tape, and they saw that Edward had come up to the apartment at nine o'clock and walked past the security desk at ten minutes after nine. He was carrying something that was wrapped in plastic and looked like it could be a painting.

"Seems way too obvious to me, Pat. Let's check the statuette for fingerprints. The kid knew he'd be on tape. Unless he just didn't care. If he didn't care, maybe there will be fingerprints. Maybe it was revenge. By now, we both know that the obvious often turns out to be fallacious and unfounded. Let's pay a visit to the son of Mr. Guy Roy. The doorman confirmed that he has moved and is living with his siblings."

The siblings were surprised to see the detectives who had to introduce themselves. Zuma reminded them that they were at their uncle Carl's funeral. Sarah kept staring at the badges and the guns in the holsters while holding on to her panda bear.

"So, the three of you drove to Guy's apartment but only you, Edward, went up? And you were there to pick up the painting of your Uncle Carl that Guy had framed?"

"Exactly, Detective, and after I brought the painting down, the three of us stopped for ice cream and went home. We hung the painting as you can see."

"Would you be willing to come down to the station for a lie detector test? We can do it at your convenience. It would be convenient for us if you could go back with us now."

"Of course, Detective Zuma. Happy to be of help in whatever ways I can."

Sarah jumped up. "Can I go too?"

"Yes, Sarah. You can go with your brother and you can even bring your panda bear. I'll let you ride in our police car and your other brother can bring along the car to take you back."

"You were right, boss. He is so willing that this obvious suspect is probably not the suspect."

"We're never right, Pat, until we are right."

CHAPTER 78

I'll Prove My Innocence

"Boss, I have never seen anyone as comfortable as he was taking the lie detector test. He was comfortable driving down, comfortable in the room, taking the test and righteous when the test confirmed that he was telling the truth about his innocence. He was smug when we told him he passed."

"He sure was, Pat. A first for us. Even innocents are nervous about taking the test. He's a strange one. Do you remember the Schnables called him an 'Iceman?' Maybe he really was guilty but eager to show us and prove to himself he was not going to fail the test and be indicted? Perhaps he could never believe that he would fail the test. He was, remember, raised by Roy and trained to control his feelings."

"But even with that, why would he be willing to take a chance?"

"At the point we showed up, he didn't have much choice. He knew we could pull him in. Maybe he thought it better to cooperate than to resist. Or call a lawyer. Maybe at that point, it didn't make a difference to him. Maybe he thought he would be able to have a good defense in court. Maybe he would be able to get his sibs to report on the short amount of time he was upstairs in the apartment and a jury would believe he would not have had the time to murder Guy. Maybe that testimony would make it difficult for a jury to convict. And maybe the other kids could testify and how calm he was when they went for ice cream. A lot of maybes...too many for us to know why he was cooperative."

"Well, if he is innocent, boss, there are only two other suspects. Both are women."

"Pat, before we jump to believing his innocence, let's figure out what he might have gained from murdering his father. And what might the two women have gained. I don't see anything that Follette could have gained so that pushes me to believe it was our furniture lady or the son."

"Do we have a record of when Sonia last saw Guy?"

"Yes, I do. But if it were her, how would she have been able to get into the building? She was not on the tape and security did not see her that evening. The coroner established the murder having occurred between eight and midnight."

"Pat, we're left with five murders and we're down to two suspects."

CHAPTER 79

A Lost Love

As she was putting Lucy down for the evening, Sonia heard the news on TV. She tried to cover the shock, but Lucy caught it and asked what the matter was.

"Sweetheart, I'm not sure but I heard the name of a man that was killed, and if I heard it correctly, I know him."

"Mommy, that is so sad. I hope you didn't hear it correctly."

"We'll let me finish putting you down. I will be fine no matter what and so will we. So, kisses to you. Let me give you an extra one tonight. Good night and sleep well."

Sonia went back in and lowered the volume.

It was definitely Guy. The cleaning lady had discovered the body and there were no suspects. She began sobbing softly. She had wanted the relationship to end but not in this abrupt manner. No goodbyes, no wishes for happiness, no possibilities for anything in the future. The announcer said that there would be a service for Mr. Roy that would be announced later in the week. The announcer then went on to cite the many things that Mr. Roy had done for the community of Santa Monica. Pictures of his stores and of the condo in Santa Monica were displayed again and again while his contributions were listed. Sonia shut the TV and got a glass of vodka, which she gulped down. She cursed quietly so Lucy would not hear. Lucy, however, was standing at the door.

"Mommy, did you know him? You must have liked him very much."

"I did, darling, I did. He was a good man who was trying to be a better father and citizen. He had learned that it was never too late to try. He is, I guess he was, like you. You try to be a good student and a good daughter."

"Mommy, but sometimes I am lazy, and I don't do all my homework or clean the dishes carefully."

"Yes, I know darling, but I know you will feel bad and the next time you will do it, you'll do it better. You never stop trying."

"That's because I want to be like you, Mommy."

Sonia started to cry again. Lucy moved towards her, gave her a hug, and kissed her on the cheek.

CHAPTER 80

Another Service

Guy's service took place in the same church that his brother was eulogized. The cast of characters was pretty much the same with a few more residents from the condo building showing up. The children were in the first pew, Sonia sat a few rows back with the detectives a few rows behind Sonia. Mary Follette was missing.

Sonia was upset that the only ones to speak were the tenants from the building and the security manager. She noticed that the children were not preparing to speak. There was no one who knew him well who was going to speak. She realized that she was the only one who could do that. She debated.

"Everyone who has spoken has said how generous Guy Roy was. I knew his generosity at a personal level. He was tremendously supportive of my art, helped me develop my websites, which helped me increase sales, which would allow me to send my daughter to study in Germany. He offered to set up a show room for my work, which seemed much too generous for me and I turned him down. In my contacts with him, he spoke kindly and affectionately about his brother Carl and his children. He always ended any discussion about his children stating how much he loved them." She made this last statement looking at Guy's children. She saw the tears in Sarah's eyes.

Zuma and Pat understood that Sonia had been speaking about her lover. Zuma admired her for the control she had in revealing as much as she could without indicating that there had been a romantic, long liaison between them. He spoke to her when she had finished and was walking out.

"I know that speaking was very hard for you."

Sonia ignored the comment and walked past Zuma and Pat without looking at them. She was not going to acknowledge a single word of his or their presence.

"Okay, Pat. Maybe Mary Follette will say a few more words than Sonia did. Let's pick her up. Don't embarrass her at work yet. Be there when she gets home."

CHAPTER 81

Stymied

Mary Follette was very cool. The two detectives told her that witnesses had seen her with Carl the night of the murder.

"Since when is being seen with someone who has been murdered evidence that a DA would believe is good enough for a trial?"

"Please go over the exact times you were with Carl, what you did, and when you left him."

"No problem, Detective Zuma."

Zuma realized, even before she recounted her story there was nothing solid for them to bring charges against her. Even if they could trace the overdose of opiates to her, which they couldn't, they had no motive.

"Pat, we are stymied. We don't know who killed Guy, and we believe that Follette killed Carl but no solid evidence."

"Boss, there is still that angry kid. We could have Milgram go back and interview him. We have no evidence on him, but we know he knew the condo pretty well. He could have gotten into the condo without being noticed,"

"Let's try that, Pat. How do we get him to go back?"

"Maybe Milgram would be willing to call him up and ask him to visit. He can say that he wants to talk about his uncle and not Guy."

"Good thinking, Pat. Can you make the call to Milgram? Tell him we would like as much information he can get about Uncle Carl."

Milgram was conflicted. He wanted to help solve the murders but couldn't quite justify doing the policemen's bidding. He resolved it by saying that he was also interested in Edward's well-being. He would just suggest an opportunity to go over the two deaths.

CHAPTER 82

Confessions to a Therapist

Milgram dropped his jaw and was speechless. He couldn't believe what he had just heard.

"I need you to repeat what you just said, Edward. Can you please do that?"

"Sure. Like I said, I know those condos back and forth. They're like a glove that fits perfectly and woven with cashmere. I slip in and out easily. Once I knew that there would be money for my siblings and especially Sarah, I felt okay about killing him. I was going to call you so when you reached out, it made it easier."

"You're confessing to a murder. Why would you do this with me instead of the police?"

"Dr. Milgram, you know me already. When I go to trial, you will be able to testify to the total abandonment by my father and his complete indifference over the years for me and my sister. The jury would be sympathetic to my having talked to you before I killed Guy. It will be better than if my defense lawyer just hired you. I have lots of money now for a good defense. And I think I can offer Zuma some information about a murderer that would be useful in establishing my cooperation in solving what has been up till now an unsolved murder."

"You know I have to report you to the police."

"Of course. I was planning to show up tomorrow morning in Detective Zuma's office. You can trust me to do that. I want to talk to my sibs about this tonight after I leave here."

"I'll trust you to show up. I was expecting this session to be about your father and your uncle. Do you want to talk about Carl?"

"No, whoever killed him will probably get what they deserve sooner or later. And maybe sooner than later. Thank you, Dr. Milgram, for your time and understanding. I think you are a good shrink. I hope my sibs will be able to use you. There's enough money for that also. Good-bye for now. I guess as the saying goes, 'I'll see you in court.'"

Milgram sat stunned. He was in shock even though his brain was racing at 100 miles an hour. He knew he had to call Zuma right away but the phrase "sooner or later" swirled in his brain. As the two words swirled, they became bigger and bigger. The word "sooner" overpowered "later." He realized that Edward was going to do something. It would not only be sooner, but it was going to be murder.

Zuma said that he was going to pick Edward up immediately and not wait for the morning. Ordinarily, Milgram would have argued to allow his client to fulfill his promise. But "sooner" washed the "ordinarily" out of his mind.

CHAPTER 83

A Falling House of Cards

Zuma was waiting for Ed when he got to the condo.

"Detective Zuma, I gather from your presence that Dr. Milgram notified you. I also want to tell you that I just killed Mary Follette. Here is the murder weapon, and I'd like to call my lawyer when you book me for the two murders. In his presence and after you book me, I will be able to give you information about two other unsolved murders one of which I did."

"Boss, I can't believe how quickly this stuff has fallen into place. The kid confesses to the Follette murder and Guy's murder and gives you solid information on Guy's murdering Hope. His explanation of that explains how Hope's roommate Lisa got killed. Lisa's murder was accidental. She was walking too closely to Hope while Hope was gunned down. Guy's moving car made it difficult to aim clearly."

"Pat, he is a shrewd cookie. Living with Guy forced him to be very observant. He worked on his intuition and did some good detective-like work. When he saw Follette at Carl's funeral, he wondered why she was there. He went to the bluffs and began describing her to the other hobos. They confirmed his images of her and said that Carl and she hung out a lot. He just decided that she was the guilty party. He didn't know what the reason might be but didn't care. He felt he was right."

"Boss, I guess he felt that another murder on top of the other two couldn't hurt him that much."

"I don't think his dying or spending the rest of his life in jail mattered to him. He cared about his siblings and as long as they were safe and comfortable, he was fine."

CHAPTER 84

Mercy and Integrity

Boss, I gotta get this straight. I need to go over this with you. Guy's son kills his father and Mary Follette. We still don't know about the Truro resident, although we think Guy or Carl or a hired person did it. That's three dead. We think Mary killed Carl, but it doesn't matter since both of them are dead. That's two more, making five dead. Guy killed Hope and Lisa. I count seven murders. We only have one suspect and that's the same one from last year and one unsolved murder. Am I right?"

"Yes, she is the suspect. And the unsolved murder is Mrs. Edna Roy."

"What do we do now?"

"Right now, we are going to have to deal with the press. I heard the news coming in to work and they are already talking about 'a serial murder,' 'a sons revenge,' and someone is playing it as a 'sibling sacrifices brother and mentally ill sister,' Those kids are going to need some protection. I hope they are up for it."

Joe realized that he and Claudia had locked horns.

"You can't go after her. If you get solid evidence and she is convicted what will happen to Lucy? There is no one else in the family. She will be handed over to foster care. And she's now a kid whose mother is a murderer. Other kids will chew her up and make mincemeat of her. She will be hounded and humiliated. That's too much for any child to handle. She has lost a father, a teacher and now could lose her mother. Joe, you need to have mercy on this kid."

"Claudia, I wish I could. I've taken an oath. I've sworn to search for the guilty. That is my job. That is what I do. I am there to ensure that the scales of justice are balanced. Murderers can't just walk around scot free."

"You need to put mercy on those scales of justice, Joe. This is not like you. This is not your best self. She's already lived two years scot free. You haven't solved the other crime that you believe she is guilty of. What is wrong with more years? Not every crime is solved."

Joe had never been confronted with anything like this in all the years he had been a detective. Someone was asking him to not pursue someone who was probably guilty. If this were a higher up, even a mayor, he would refuse to accept that directive. But this was Claudia, the woman he loved.

"Joe, if you go forward, I will seek to adopt her. If she comes into our life, she will never accept you. She will come between us. Please don't do this. She is an innocent. Not an innocent adult who can eventually understand but an innocent child."

"Claudia, you're making me choose between you and my integrity."

"In my eyes you would have more integrity if you give up your pursuit. Your integrity will include mercy."

CHAPTER 85

Saving a Life

He was not sleeping well and was irritable and short with Claudia. She was patient with him, realizing how difficult it was for him to have seen the world through the eyes of a child rather than through his career eyes. She marveled that he was able to keep wrestling with the issue of whether he had done right or wrong.

"Joe, remember when you told me how angry you were that your wife got killed? Suppose you had done something in revenge, and you were sent away. What do you think that would have done to your children, knowing that their father murdered someone?"

"I can only imagine. It would have been horrendous. It probably would have wrecked their lives."

"Yes, and you would have been haunted by the idea of what you had done to your children. I believe that Sonia must sometimes feel the same way."

"Maybe you're right. I wish I knew that."

"Your guilty party did something out of revenge. What you're doing now is preventing a life from being wrecked."

The end of school was approaching. Claudia was having her students finish up their projects. Lucy was going to go off to Germany with the Schnables, and Joe and Claudia were getting ready to go back to the Cape for their two-week vacation with his boys arriving during their second week.

"Goodbye, Claudia. Will you be here next year when I come back to school? I want you to be here so I can take more classes with you."

"Yes, I will, Lucy. But, if for some reason I'm not, I will make sure that you visit me where I am living."

Sonia felt something was different in the way Zuma was looking at her when he showed up for the goodbyes of teachers, parents, and students.

He seemed to be less focused on her and more on the students, especially Lucy. She hoped she would be able to worry less about his pursuit of justice. If he could drop that she thought it would be a chance for her to make a better life. She would be getting a second chance because of Lucy.

CHAPTER 86

Cape Cod

Joe received an e mail form Pat when they arrived at the Cape.

> I know you're on holiday, but I want to let you know that you are my "Tambourine Man and I will always be following you." You never have to 'think twice" because you usually get it right, right, right away. Have a great holiday and be "Forever Young."

Joe smiled deeply.

It took them a few days to settle into their routines: Claudia painting, Joe catching fresh fish or digging for clams and cooking, and Claudia and Joe both finding theater and plays in P Town. But they each felt a difference in themselves about the other. Claudia knew how much Joe had changed in his basic beliefs about justice. She knew that he changed because of her. That he now saw more of the world as she did made her feel close to him in a way that she never realized was possible. Joe knew that what felt at first like giving up something was in fact a set of gains. He had gained a view of mercy, a view of the world as a child sees it and the surety that these gains created bonds between them that would never be broken. His dad was right, "Everyone deserves a second chance."